SACRIFICE ISLAND

by Kristin Dearborn

Dedication

To Steve B, who decided that two weeks in Palawan was an excellent idea.
Also for being a most excellent friend.

Acknowledgements

First round of thanks go to Steve B, Ruban, and Warren, who were with me on an inspirational adventure to the Philippines. Steve meticulously planned our routes and travel, so all I had to do was show up and enjoy.

The next round goes to my beta readers: Mom, Christina, Brian, Steve and Mac. They read the book before you did, and pointed out parts that maybe didn't work so well. Thanks to Dave at DarkFuse, who taught me the difference between "that" and "which." I've taken your Post-It suggestion to heart. Big thanks to Tony Masia, David Dodd and David Wilson and the rest of the gang at Crossroad Press, who saw the opportunity to revive *Sacrifice Island* like a phoenix rising from the flames.

Thanks to supportive friends, who stand by as I write, and to everyone at Seton Hill, who have always pushed me to be better. Thank you to Scott, the strongest, bravest guy I know. Thanks to Karen, for letting me use her name.

Prologue

"How about the special tour? After dark only."

Marissa's head spun and she giggled. Colored light spilled from the bar to illuminate their patch of beach. Reds, greens, and blues winked on the calm seawater.

Her companion, a tall German whose name she couldn't remember, asked, "What is this special tour?"

The boatman's white smile glowed in the moonlight. Marissa remembered him from earlier in the day. He'd driven the boat she and her friend took to visit some of the nearby beaches. Low on personality, high on competence.

"He was my guide this afternoon, he's cool," she whispered to the German. He hushed her.

"How much?"

"Eight hundred pesos."

"The price is steep. Where do you take us?"

"Past Helicopter Island. To a beach not on any of the maps."

"Why isn't it on the maps?" Marissa and Suzanne spent ten and a half months planning this trip. Marissa saved and scrimped to get here, but Suzanne's dad paid her way. Marissa'd pushed for the Caribbean—much closer (and cheaper), or for Thailand— more developed, more to do. But Suzanne convinced her, and she'd gotten a night job at a grocery store, stocking shelves. She deposited all the proceeds in a jar marked "Palawan."

And now they were here. It was every bit as beautiful as Suzanne had assured her it would be. Six daiquiris later, she couldn't feel her sunburn anymore. She'd loved the limestone islands by day, towering karst cliffs and jagged rocks, beaches with sand as white and fine as flour. The best part? Palawan was still mostly off the beaten path, a South Pacific paradise. It wasn't trashed like the beaches in Thailand. She couldn't help wonder…what would the islands from this afternoon look like in the moonlight?

The guide answered her question. "It's not on any maps because it is a special place. Tourists bring litter and damage the corals."

"Can we do a night dive?" Marissa asked.

"You're drunk." The German kissed the top of her head. They met on the bus from Puerto Princesa yesterday afternoon.

"So're you."

"Let's just go for a swim."

"A swim on a secret island. Let's go."

The German frowned at the guide. "The price is high."

"I'll pay for it. I want to go." She leaned in, close to his ear. "I bet he won't care if we fuck on the beach." If only she could remember his name. It wasn't a super-German name like Hans, or Lars…what was it?

"If you want to." He carefully pronounced the words against alcohol. "I don't have so much money left."

"Don't worry about it." To the guide she said, "We'll go."

The guide grinned wide in the moonlight. "Bring a sweat-shirt. The ride across the bay can be cold at night."

Marissa hadn't brought a sweatshirt, but her German did, and they both huddled inside it, stretching the material. The ocean spray, refreshing in the ninety-degree afternoon sunlight, chilled her in the glow of the moon.

"Don't worry," the guide said from behind them, where he sat by the loud motor. Flimsy pontoons jutted from either side of the boat. It was painted white with a seafoam green interior that became dark in the moonlight. The name *Baby Roxanne* stood out on the hull in fuchsia paint. All vehicles here—trikes, boats, trucks—were named, and half of the names seemed to include *Baby*. Crowded in with eleven people, the boat felt cramped and claustrophobic. Now it seemed massive, as she and the German (*what, what, what was his name?*) huddled on one of the long, empty benches.

This afternoon's ride took almost an hour coming back against the wind. Tonight's would be farther. Marissa shivered, thankful for the German's warmth. She wished she wore more than her bikini and a sarong converted into a halter dress. Back at the beachfront bar she'd been plenty warm.

She resisted the urge to ask the guide how much farther. Maybe this wasn't such a great idea. She suspected Suzanne wasn't shivering. When Marissa last saw her at the bar, she'd been flirting with an Australian surfer and a redheaded British girl. Marissa leaned into her German.

Marissa woke to a sudden silence as the guide killed *Baby Roxanne*'s engine.

"We're here."

She must have dozed off. He dropped the wooden stairs into the water with a splash. The *Baby Roxanne* rocked in gentle waves, moored in a cove protected from the wind. Here the sea lapped a luminous beach with gentle kisses. The moon pulled all color from the vista, but replaced it with a blue filter that gave everything a magical mood. With no light pollution, a million stars glittered in the sky, the thick band of the Milky Way clearly visible. She saw Orion, just like at home.

Warm calf-deep water, still heated from a day in the baking tropical sun, lapped at Marissa's legs. She waded to shore, and sunk her toes into the cool sand. Her German followed.

Their guide, perched on the seafoam green bow of the boat, pointed behind them.

They turned. So beautiful! Nestled in a shallow cave stood a statue of the Virgin Mary, her hands holding a giant clam, eyes demurely lowered. Her marble edifice seemed to glow with its own light.

"There's more." The guide pointed at the dark jungle. He lit a cigarette and settled onto his haunches.

Squinting in the moonlight, Marissa saw more marble, dappled with shadows. She took the German's hand and squeezed. He smiled at her. They went forward to explore.

The guide watched them go. He took a long pull on his cigarette and rubbed at his chin. The girl's peal of loud laugher rolled across the water.

They spoke to each other in hushed tones. He couldn't make out words, but he heard her voice, then his, then hers again... back and forth. Sound carried far on a calm night like this one.

From a ways off, the girl gasped. The sound echoed up the limestone cliffs. The guide smiled. Not a gasp of pleasure—he'd heard them discuss having relations on the beach. Neither of them would ever have relations again.

Not even enough time to smoke a full cigarette. *She* was hungry tonight. The German shouted, terror in his voice, and the girl screamed, a high, pure sound. *"No, no, no!"* The sound rolled across the water. The girl's voice was lovely. The guide carefully extinguished his cigarette so he could finish it later, and tucked the remnants behind his ear.

As the man's screams joined the woman's, the guide poled away from the beach, into deeper water. With two good tugs, he started the outboard motor. The roar almost drowned out the screams. They were fading, anyway. He turned into the breeze, and headed for home.

One

The piano paused as Alex let himself into the apartment. He plopped down in an overstuffed chair to listen. Jemma sat at her piano, dressed in black, her rod-straight back to him. He didn't recognize the piece; something classical, impossibly complex sounding. He, a Luddite, would never even hope to play like she did. He'd never progressed much past "Heart and Soul"—both parts—on the piano.

She'd left him a voice mail, breathless and excited. He should come over after he got out of work: she'd found the fourth chapter for the book.

Gray light from the window made her pale skin glow. He watched her long, thin fingers, her skinny wrists. She wore gloves whenever she went out, seeing her fingers was scandalous, like seeing a Victorian's ankle. He watched the way her hands peeked out of baggy sleeves to flit over the piano keys. She wore a long, flowing black garment; from here he couldn't tell if it was pants or a skirt. Her shirt was more of the same. Believe it or not, this was an improvement. She bought a pair of jeans recently. She didn't dare wear them, but she owned them, and he was proud of her.

She finished with no flourish. She would never be a great pianist because she didn't insert any of herself into the music. She could recreate the sounds perfectly, but Jemma Labasan was never present in the melodies.

"I know what we'll do for the last chapter." She beamed at him from behind a shank of black, silky hair. She wore it long, a fence between herself and the world. Her few years growing up in Britain, as well as her parents' accents, left the slightest lilt to her words as she spoke.

"Great!" Alex also dug up a pretty great last chapter, right here in New York.

"I found a journal," she said.

So far, off to a good start. Journals made for good beginnings.

"Her name was Rebecca St. Germaine. She had an abusive husband, but he died—"

Alex studied her. Would this hit too close to home?

"—and after his death she went to an island. It wasn't a convent, not exactly, but it is a holy Catholic place, with shrines and a dormitory. The journal shows her slowly going mad and being enticed by spirits on the island! Then she killed herself!"

Alex listened and it all sounded promising. He could tell, though, this wasn't the whole story.

"Where's the island?"

"The book is called *Spirits Around the World*, right?"

Where did she want them to go? They'd been to England, to Canada, up to New England for chapters. Her evasiveness suggested somewhere more exotic.

Jemma drifted to the table to get her laptop. She never merely walked anywhere. She moved with the grace of a dancer, and the way her clothes flowed around her made her seem to float. She handed the computer to him, careful their hands didn't touch.

He saw images of palm trees, cerulean skies, turquoise water, and white sand. Beautiful. Hell yes he wanted to go there. But...

"You hate the heat. And the sun. And you hate bugs. Jem, are you sure this is a good idea? Where is this?"

"The island is called Palawan. In the Philippines."

"Jesus, that's like, twenty-four hours on an airplane. Security's going to touch you."

"Maybe not."

"Maybe not," he agreed, though he remembered what happened when they had.

Outside, sleet tinged against the window of Jemma's cozy one-bedroom apartment. Wet slush and ice drenched New York. Alex allowed himself to fantasize about tropical sunlight baking his skin, the feel of hot sand under his bare feet, and bathwater warm seas. He'd been to Florida once, and couldn't imagine what this paradise would be like. He clicked through some more pictures. Heaven.

Jemma's hands, porcelain white and painfully thin, would burn in the tropical sun.

"Can you fund it?" She peered at him, unable to keep a smile off her lips.

Alex could write a grant better than anyone she knew. He bragged he could fund anything, and so far he'd never been proven wrong. "Of course I can get funding."

"I want to go for a month."

He breathed out a puff of air. "Okay, start at the top. What's the ghost?"

In Connecticut, they visited a haunted boarding school. In Canada, a haunted forest that turned out to be a hoax. For the England trip they visited a haunted castle, which would sound like a cliché, but actually had been the stuff nightmares were made of.

"Our Lady of Perpetual Sorrows shrine on Sakripisiyuhin Island."

"*What* island?"

"It's a mouthful, eh? Means 'Sacrifice' in Tagalog. People used to go there to pray and feel closer to God. Rebecca and four other women killed themselves there in '94. It closed, and tourists stopped visiting. Locals won't go near it."

"And ghosts?"

"How can there not be ghosts?"

"You want to head to the other side of the world because there are *probably* ghosts there?" To be fair, there probably were ghosts there.

She lighted on the chair opposite him.

"In her diary she described spirits coaxing her to do sinful things."

Alex wondered what kind of sinful things, and if maybe Jemma simply stumbled onto some kind of weird *Letters to Penthouse.*

"It's every bit as sordid as you're imagining."

Alex chuckled. How well she knew him.

"Have you found recent intel on this?"

"No, no one goes there."

"What if we don't find anything?"

Alex wanted to go, simply because he'd love to have a trip to a place like this, like Palawan. But he didn't much look forward to getting there, finding nothing of interest to Jemma, and heading back early.

"You're going to hate it, you know?" He decided to be blunt. "People will think you dress funny."

"I do dress funny. Read the diary," she said. She studied him with big brown eyes. "And it'll be a wonderful holiday for you. We can come back before a month if we need to. I feel—I really think this will be good. That it will make a good addition to the book."

"All right," Alex said. Canada had been similar; Jemma insisted they go. He'd had a hard time finding anything about the place she'd chosen. Yes, the ghost part wound up being a hoax, but their investigation provided key details that helped solve a park ranger's murder. Jemma was *sensitive,* and if she said they needed to go to the Philippines, then he believed her. She'd never led him astray.

Yet.

Two

Terry Brenton made his way down the crowded side street, breathing dust and dodging vehicles. A garishly painted trike—the *Carla Baby*—nearly struck him as it wove around a parked delivery truck. A couple nearly walked into him, an average looking middle-aged white man and a pixie like Filipino girl. Terry used to love El Nido, but sometimes...

He pushed away fantasies of leaving, of heading back to the UK. He didn't have children there, or any family left, but it was home. Sometimes even the hot air and the palm trees and the cerulean seas all made him miss the drab, gray, dreary weather he grew up with.

All around him stood buildings converted to guesthouses, painted in bright colors to attract backpackers. He passed massage parlors (some of them reputable, some of them not), stalls that sold bootleg DVDs and cheap plastic toys, little restaurants, the signs all in English. Like it or not, this was home now.

He paused in front of Louie's Backyard, the best place to get a drink on the island. Downstairs hosted a gift shop packed with expensive Palawan and El Nido souvenirs, upstairs sat the bar and café. Terry trotted up the stairs. Even five years ago such an endeavor wouldn't have made his heart pound. He felt old.

The owner of Louie's Backyard was no Louie, but an American named Erica. She sat at the edge of the balcony, a sloe gin fizz parked in front of her. She rarely could be found without one, never drunk, always sipping.

"Terry! Just the man I wanted to see," she called, her voice a welcoming smoker's growl.

He waved, ordered an old-fashioned from a shy Filipina at

the bar, then made his way to the balcony to join Erica. She hailed from Cleveland or someplace comparably dreadful.

"Good afternoon." Terry dropped into a plastic chair.

"There's a pair of paranormal investigators on their way up here from Puerto Princesa."

"Paranormal whats?"

"Ghost hunters. They're going to check out the island. They got some kind of a grant from the University of Oregon."

Terry's drink came. His heart pounded. Goddammit. He couldn't have people out there, poking around.

"They made me think of Virginia."

Terry's chest clenched—a merciful heart attack? Then he wouldn't need to worry about any of this.

He plastered a smile on his face.

"Where will they stay?"

"Not sure. Maria down in Puerto said they took the eleven o'clock up here, so they'll arrive sometime in the next"—she checked a thin, expensive watch—"half hour? Hour? Depends on the roads and how the lunch stop went."

Terry hoped no one could see his sweat. He had the van; he could be at the bus terminal to meet them when their Jeepney arrived.

"Do you want to host the ghost hunters? Have some problems at the resort?" She laughed at her own joke, but her eyes remained serious.

"I'll keep them in line," he said.

"Is there anyone still around who was there in the nineties?"

"Not that I know of." Most of them had gone home. Not Virginia. She stayed, and they opened a resort together. Had many wonderful years on the beach.

A pair of tattooed Australian girls trotted up the stairs. Erica saw her bartender had vanished and hefted herself up from her patch of sun to tend to them.

"Have fun with the ghost hunters. Keep a good eye on them, Terry."

He waved and hurried down to his van. He racked his brain about whether there were rooms available. He pulled out his cell phone and called the resort restaurant. Anna answered, his right-hand woman.

She spoke, always, in a polite, accented monotone. She ran the kitchen and all the housekeeping for the past three years, and the entire resort would have been defunct without her.

"What're the best cabins we have available?"

Any of the other staff would have had to go and check. Anna paused for a split second. "Two and six," she said.

"Keep them empty until I get back."

"Yes, sir. Anything else, sir?"

He used to think she mocked him with her monotone and aggressive use of "sir" and "ma'am." He'd come to accept her way of being polite.

Terry parked at the El Nido bus terminal. A Crayola spread of color painted the sky. A wonderful first impression of the Vista Breeze resort.

Terry watched and waited.

Three

The Jeepney arrived in El Nido at dusk. As soon as the brightly colored vehicle came to a stop, passengers flooded out onto the dusty parking lot: the El Nido bus terminal. Alex sat tight and waited for them all to go. He shielded Jemma, who sat hunched as close to the wall as she could manage, her straw purse held as a barrier between them. He never imagined so many people could pack themselves into a vehicle this size. For a few miles from the middle of nowhere to Roxas, there had even been three men hanging on the outside.

Jemma disembarked last. She watched as two native men hefted her black Pelican cases from the roof of the van. The cases contained their gear: laptops, recording devices, ectometers.

If Alex was hot—and he was—Jemma must be dying. She wore a loose-fitting long-sleeved black T-shirt and flowing black pants that hid the fact she even had two legs. On her head she wore a wide straw hat. Light silk gloves covered her hands. She allowed Alex to talk her out of getting a black one. Her big, dark sunglasses made her look like she was trying to hide from someone.

"Pardon me?"

The voice sounded like C-3PO: a neat, prissy, insufferable British accent. Alex ignored it, certain the chap couldn't possibly be talking to them.

"Do these crates belong to you?" he went on, caught Jemma's eye, and pointed at the cases around her feet.

"Yes," she said, barely more than mumbling.

The speaker was tall and thin, with sandy hair heading over to white and a bristly mustache. He wore a light cotton shirt, red and blue plaid faded to pastel. He coupled it with khaki shorts.

The man perused Alex and Jemma. "Are you folks the..." His voice trailed off. "Are you here to..." He pursed his lips and made a little sucking sound. Alex grinned. Uncomfortable people were so much fun.

"Are you here to visit the island?" he asked.

"We are," said Jemma. Alex laughed.

The Brit extended his hand to Jemma, but Alex intercepted for her and introduced them.

"I'm Terry Brenton. Pleased to meet you." Terry shook hands with a tentative, dry grip. "I'm the proprietor of Vista Breeze resort. Have you found accommodations here in El Nido?"

Jemma deferred to Alex. He'd read about this place online. There were loads of boardinghouses and resorts in the area, but he seemed to recall this one came highly recommended.

"I don't want to swindle you, or put one over on you. I have a certain interest in Sakripisiyuhin Island, and hoped I could be of some help to your project."

Jemma lifted her chin. Alex hoped Vista Breeze—and what the hell kind of name was that, anyway?—sat on the more affordable end of the spectrum.

"All right," Jemma said.

"I have two cottages available—or do you only need one?"

Alex and Jemma stepped away from each other. "Two, please," they said in unison.

Terry regarded them strangely—can't a man and woman travel together without the world assuming they're screwing? (Answer: no.) "Well, the cottages are oceanfront, and they're free—unoccupied, I mean—for the duration of your stay. I've my van here now, and could take you and your things."

Instinct told Alex to shop around. The offer right off the bus couldn't possibly be the best one. Jemma fanned herself. He could see dark pockets of sweat under her armpits, and heavy dark circles sat under her eyes. She started to consent, and he cut her off.

"How did you hear about us? How'd you know we'd be here?"

Terry smiled, a mouthful of surprisingly white teeth that

stood out against his tanned face. "This island is a small, quiet place. Word traveled quickly about two writers with a grant to come here. When I heard the project involved Sakripisiyuhin Island, why, I wanted to do everything I could to help out."

Red flags triggered in Alex's head. He was exceptional at reading people, which Jemma told him was a sixth sense of a kind. He chose to believe he was just perceptive.

"And what's your interest in the place?"

Jemma sagged on the cases in the setting sun, and here they stood in the middle of a dusty parking lot. The other passengers had already taken waiting vans or trikes to their accommodations. Alex envisioned a shower, and a cocktail overlooking the water. Then a delicious, locally caught fish for dinner.

Terry's smile only widened. "I could talk about the island for hours. My wife stayed there for a short while. We loved it there. I want to be sure you do the place right. It's not all tragedy, you know."

Despite Terry's sincere tone, he cut his eyes to the left as he said the last bit. Strange. "Last question. What's your charge for the rooms?"

"Fifteen hundred pesos a night. Air-conditioned, close to the beach, Wi-Fi in the restaurant when there's power. We've got power in El Nido from two p.m. until six a.m. Some of the restaurants or bars in town have generators, but for the most part, during the day, there's nothing."

Alex turned to Jemma. He wished he could see her eyes. He lifted his shoulder, asking her what she thought. She gave the tiniest nod. It all sounded fine. Terry helped load the cases into the back of the van. He scurried around to the driver's seat. Alex let Jemma have shotgun. She stared out the window, away from Terry, as they drove. They passed striking limestone cliffs, jungle, and small shacks. Chickens scampered into the road, but managed to avoid getting hit. Mangy dogs watched them from shadows on the side of the road. Alex chatted about El Nido, and the restaurant's menu for tonight. The ride took less than ten minutes. Terry told them they had the best of both worlds—relatively easy access to the town and all its conveniences, but Vista Breeze sat far enough away that the nights were quiet.

"Always wear shoes," Terry told them. "Rockfish, stinging coral, jellyfish...but it's infection you have to worry the most about. These are the tropics."

Alex smiled politely, but could see Jemma's profile reflected in the window. She frowned at the passing scenery. The van bumped and jostled them down a rutted dirt road. They drove a bit, then began to pass charming little cottages. When Terry parked the van next to the restaurant, they stepped out to their first good view of the sea. Sunset painted the calm water in various shades of red, orange and yellow. Canoes with outriggers dotted the water line, and a few people waded in shallow water.

The restaurant sat on the second floor. They took their shoes off at the door as was customary. White sand stood out against Jemma's dark socks.

"Come up to the restaurant to check in. We can get those rooms squared away."

Jemma looked back at the pile of gear, as though willing it to still be there when they got back, then followed Terry though a rustic sitting room with many pieces of Molave wood furniture. They headed up the stairs to a lovely open-air bar perched over a picturesque beach. In the dying light of sunset, the tall palm fronds framing the sea stood out as black silhouettes. Fuck chasing ghosts, this was fantastic.

Terry prattled on about laundry, about a cage they kept on the property housing Palawan bearcats.

"What's a bearcat?" Jemma asked.

Terry brightened. "Follow me!" And before they could argue, he hurried down the stairs. They followed. Alex and Jemma kicked on their shoes and followed Terry out into a darkness punctuated by cheery holiday lights. Around the back of the bar sat a cage about the size of one of the little cabins. Terry flicked a switch and two incandescent bulbs came to life. Inside the cage were walkways and branches, loads of things to climb on. On a shelf up near the top sat two furry balls. One remained stationary, apparently uninterested in them, but the other unfurled, stretched, and waddled down a branch to investigate.

"That's Mantikayla. That's Binusang up there, but he isn't so friendly."

Mantikayla looked like a long black raccoon. Her curious little feet pawed at Jemma through the wire of the cage. Her long eyebrows and whiskers were almost white, and she had a white diamond on her chest they could see when she stood on her hind feet. Her prehensile tail stretched almost as long as her body.

"Want to go in?" Terry asked.

"Are they friendly?" Alex wasn't sure about the one with the B name. Every so often he'd pop his head up, flick his ears, then go back to sleep.

"Yes, please!"

Jemma could touch animals. She loved their contact and their company.

Terry let her in. "Be careful. Those two are escape artists."

Jemma kneeled down, and Mantikayla climbed on her leg and sniffed for treats. "She smells like popcorn!" Jemma said.

"Weird."

"Her name means 'butter' in Tagalog. His name means 'popcorn.'"

"Do you want to go in?" Terry asked Alex.

"No thanks."

Alex waited patiently for a few more minutes. Terry handed Jemma a piece of mango to feed the bearcat. Popcorn stood and waddled down a branch, but he kept his distance, blinking at them with red-brown eyes.

"Let's go see our rooms. We can come play with these guys later," he finally said.

Mantikayla finished her fruit, Jemma gave her a few parting scratches, and Terry opened the door.

"What about Sacrifice Island?" Jemma asked, as they took off their shoes again to head inside.

"You'll have to charter a boat. Most of the guides won't go there."

She smiled at him. "Is it really so frightening?"

"No." Terry bolstered his words with a laugh, but Alex noticed again how his eyes cut left while he spoke of the island.

"Who do you suggest we get to charter? We'd like to head out there tomorrow, if it's possible."

"You don't want a day to rest first?"

Terry didn't want them going out there. Alex could tell. It lay buried in his voice; in the way he played with the frayed edge of his shirt, where he cast his gaze.

"We want to go in the daylight, get a feel for the place. Nothing major, we won't even bring the gear this time."

A beautiful Filipina woman appeared behind the bar. The way her hair hung in her face reminded Alex of Jemma, but this woman radiated defiant fire.

"This is Anna, my right-hand woman."

Anna said nothing.

"Can you charter Mr. Lucky for tomorrow?"

She nodded, then vanished on silent, bare feet.

"All set," Terry said, without waiting to hear anything back from Anna. "He'll be here at nine."

"You're sure?"

"Positive. Mr. Lucky would never let me down." He gave them an encouraging smile, but it came across as flat and hollow, setting Alex's Spidey senses tingling again.

"Anna! Get me the keys to two and six, please!"

Alex examined Anna when she came back with the keys. She wasn't terribly tall, a slender, delicate frame. Thick bangs hemmed in her beautiful face, too heavy for her delicate features. Her eyes were her most striking feature, light tan and so serious. Alex scoped out her ass, hugged in a pair of well-fitting sweatpants, and her honey-colored skin. She handed off the keys without a glance at Alex or Jemma.

Cabins two and six. Alex kept the key to two for himself, and handed six to Jemma. She smiled. Six was her lucky number.

Four

Jemma tossed and turned all night long. Once the air conditioner shut off with the power at six a.m., she gave up all hopes of sleep. Outdoor sounds flooded in—roosters announcing the new day, barking dogs, playing children, boat motors. It wasn't disagreeable, simply impossible to sleep through. So Jemma got up. The cabin was pleasant enough: the floors clean, the bed reasonably comfortable. The bathroom was small, but it contained a toilet—which Alex warned her might be a rarity in this part of the world. The shower consisted of a spigot sticking out of the wall in a tiled bathroom. It didn't much matter what got wet and what didn't. A little metal shield protected the toilet paper.

Outside, a gray predawn light bathed the beach and jungle. Jemma shrugged on a flowing black dress and stepped into her flip-flops. Each cabin had a tiny front porch with a Molave table and two matching chairs. The furniture followed the contours of the natural wood, making it lumpy and misshapen—but in beautiful way: tropical and wild.

Low tide left its impressions on the sand, as Jemma stared out at Corong-Corong beach.

The boat wouldn't be here until ten; plenty of time to explore and reread some of the diary. She kept her flip-flops on, as Terry suggested. After his warning, she expected things to surge out of the mud to spear and infect her feet. In a shallow lake at the end of a strange track sat a starfish. Those, she was pretty sure, weren't poisonous. It was tan and gray and nondescript. Poisonous things were usually flamboyant and colorful. She gently scooped a hand under it, lifting it out of the sand and water. The tips of its five legs curled up and revealed confused, waving suckers underneath.

One of the resort's not quite stray dogs hovered nearby, plumy tail waving, thinking perhaps this strange woman had food.

Jemma returned the starfish to the shallow, sandy sea. She found another nearby, then another, then another, and realized the beach swarmed with them. She felt a bit foolish for her earlier enthusiasm.

She walked to where sand bars ended and the sea began. She dipped her toes in the lapping shallow water, held up her skirt, and gazed at the little boats moored there. Fishermen boarded their crafts, men and children walked on the beach. The dogs raced and played, snapping and barking at one another.

Jemma made her way back to shore, back to the restaurant to find some breakfast. Alex could sleep through anything, and she didn't expect him until after nine, when they'd agreed to meet. She reviewed the notes they'd collected as she waited.

Sometime during the Second World War an American soldier found a spring on the island which he said ran red, like Christ's blood. The island was forgotten for years until a small group of Catholics, some Filipinos, some Japanese, mostly French, came to believe Sakripisiyuhin Island was a sacred place, hidden away from the world, untouched and unspoiled by the savagery of man. The spring, they said, ran red on religiously significant days.

In 1980 a wealthy French businessman decided to build a shrine there, importing marble from Makrana, India, shaping the stone into several statures of the Virgin Mary. Day-trippers would come to quietly pray and meditate under her watchful gaze. A marble gazebo in an archaic Greek style and a dormitory for wayward travelers followed in 1985. The elusive red spring proved hard to find. Every few years someone would mention finding it, and then it would disappear for a decade or more.

Sacrifice Island became a popular tourist attraction for visitors from El Nido—not that tourism was a big draw here in those days. Word of the area's beauty spread, and for almost fifteen years, the island held its place as a quirky religious site. There was some trouble at the dormitory, sure...a few suicides, but this was almost to be expected considering many of the girls who were sent there were troubled to begin with. Rebecca's diary detailed some of these occurrences.

In 1994 the suicides spiked, culminating with a public self-immolation, and Sacrifice Island vanished from the day-tour circuit. After the spate of suicides, including Rebecca's, the Catholics and tourists alike abandoned the island and it fell back into obscurity. There were reports of strange deaths in El Nido for the next year—1995—but after that, things calmed down. A few more disappearances than normal, but El Nido was an end-of-the-road kind of place for a lot of folks. Come here with what money they had left, and when it runs out...vanish. The island had been abandoned for eighteen years.

Around 8:40, Alex blundered up the stairs and ordered bacon and eggs.

Terry walked the beach, out for a morning stroll. "Something about him," said Alex. "He doesn't want us on the island."

Jemma perked up. "Then there must be something there."

Terry headed toward the restaurant.

"We know there's *something* there. It's a matter of what."

Jemma watched the shifting sea, and Alex ate his breakfast.

Terry plopped down at their table with a cheerful "Good morning!"

Alex, still half-asleep, mumbled the same. Jemma smiled.

"Excited for your first go with the island?" he asked.

They nodded. It seemed uncouth to express the same level of enthusiasm as Terry.

"Will you spend the night in the dormitory?"

Jemma smiled politely. "I'm afraid not. Not tonight, anyway. We're taking a few hours to get a feel for the place. Not even bringing our gear. We're going to see what we feel and notice."

Terry frowned. "Most of the action happens at night, does it not?"

"What do you mean, action?" Alex tried to drill in, get Terry to spill something that might help.

"I just assumed that ghosts...night...isn't that when they

come out?" He tripped over his words. Alex caught a delicious chill. So there was something out there. It was nice to feel like he hadn't traveled to the other side of the world for nothing.

"We need the lay of the land," Alex said. "Stumbling around at night wouldn't be terribly productive. There's energy around all the time. We'll pick something up."

Terry looked a bit deflated.

"I'm sure we'll have an overnight sooner or later," Alex said.

"I'd think sooner would get faster results."

"That's the thing about those ghost-hunting shows. They only feature the payoff, not the weeks or months of research."

"Months?"

"Sometimes," Alex said. Jemma smiled. This must have been an easier endeavor back before everyone considered themselves amateur paranormal investigators.

"How long do you plan to stay here?"

"A month," said Alex.

"As long as it takes," said Jemma.

Terry looked from one of them to the other. He paused, and Jemma watched Alex read his silence. "Brilliant! This is your home away from home as long as you need it!"

"Much obliged," Alex said. Jemma could tell he was waking up, gathering his wits. He scrutinized Terry. "Have you lost your wife?"

The color drained from Terry's face, and he lowered his eyes to his wedding band, which he'd been playing with all morning.

"How did you know?"

Alex shrugged. "A feeling I got," he said.

Jemma stayed quiet.

"You can...see things?"

"Only sometimes," Alex lied. "I mean, I know stuff sometimes. Glimpses. It's been a while, hasn't it?"

"Four years next month." He nodded.

"I'm so sorry," Jemma interjected. Alex amazed her with what he could discover.

Terry stood and went to the railing overlooking the sea. "Your boat is here."

Alex changed the subject. "Did you have a hard time finding

someone who'd take us to the island?"

"Not really. I know who to ask. Not everyone thinks it's a dark place. I've been out several times and it can be quite pleasant."

"Did you ever feel anything strange, anything *off*, no matter how quiet, how simple?" Jemma asked.

"Never." Jemma watched Alex watch him. His eyes narrowed, just for a moment. They bid Terry good-bye and headed off down the stairs.

"What are you doing?" Jemma asked.

"Every so often," Alex kept his voice quiet, "ole Terry lies to us. He's incredibly bad at it. I had his tell figured within five minutes of meeting the man. He's felt something on the island, seen something. I'm sure of it."

"How did you know about his wife?"

"He plays with the band when he gets nervous. He didn't mention her. If she'd left him, he wouldn't still wear the ring. Bonine?" Alex pulled the motion-sickness tablets out of his pack.

Since this was a day trip, they only took Alex's backpack full of sunscreen, towels and other mundane beach-combing paraphernalia.

A large Filipino, his skin dark from the sun, tightened ropes on the canoe, a teal vessel with the name *Baby Roxanne* painted in pink letters on its hull.

He turned and regarded them, then tossed a cigarette butt into the water. He grinned at them, and Jemma felt her soul grow dark.

Five

Goose bumps rose all over Jemma's skin, and she studied the guide's leering face. She sunk behind Alex.

The boatman grinned at them, showcasing a gold tooth, and he jutted out a big hand. "I am Mr. Lucky." He pronounced "mister" as "mistah." He sized up her unorthodox outfit, she could tell he thought she was a freak. It was okay, everyone did.

"And are you?" Alex shook the offered hand.

"Am I what?" Mr. Lucky's thick accent proved easy to understand.

"Are you lucky?"

He leered again, his devil grin. "Oh, yes, sir."

They paused for a moment, anticipating more information of some kind. When none came, Jemma followed Alex and Mr. Lucky through the ankle-deep ocean. The boat looked like it was moored in deep water, but even out this far, the water only lapped at their knees. Jemma hiked up her skirts. The hem still managed to get wet.

"Sakripisiyuhin Island, you want?"

"Yes, sir," Alex said.

Jemma declined Mr. Lucky's extended hand and hauled herself up the little ladder onto the boat. Alex dropped onto the bench under the canopy. The *Baby Roxanne* comfortably seated ten. Jemma positioned herself as close to the front of the boat as she could get while staying out of the sun. The *Baby Roxanne* was painted a brilliant shade of teal, made paler by the blue of the sky, and the blue sea stretching out all around them.

Jemma would have found it beautiful, if not for the man on the boat with them. She could never relax, could never appreciate the vista in Mr. Lucky's company.

The boatman poled them into deeper water. Other tours left all around them, smiling tourists with diving fins and snorkels. All the other tour boats had two guides...why didn't theirs? Out in deeper water Mr. Lucky settled himself, and the quiet morning exploded with the shotgun sound of the motor.

"Whisper quiet!" Alex shouted.

Jemma favored him with a weak smile. She crossed her arms over her chest and stared anywhere but at Mr. Lucky. His negativity washed over her, crept into her pores, wrapped her and caressed her.

The ride started smooth, but as they left the shelter of nearby islands, the water changed from teal to a steely blue much more familiar to New Yorkers. Alex pointed out flying fish. White caps tipped some of the waves and the little vessel rocked back and forth, its pontoons slapping the water.

Jemma held the side of the boat and willed the ride to end. She didn't like boats. As a girl she'd hated motorboat rides on Lake Winnipesaukee with her uncle. Eventually, after years of whining, they'd let her stay at his lakeside house instead, free to peruse her aunt's collection of Time Life books detailing the unexplained. Her mother still blamed Aunt Lottie for her interest in ghosts.

Jemma could feel Mr. Lucky watching her, and despite the heat, she wished she wore even more clothes, anything to make herself disappear under his watchful eye. She stole a glance at Alex, who seemed to enjoy the sea spray and lovely weather.

The ride dragged on, and she resisted the urge to look at the time. She tried to focus on the project at hand, the spirit that plagued Sakripisiyuhin Island. She wondered about the island's history before the European Catholics arrived. Alex pointed, and she followed the direction of his finger. Ahead of them loomed a tall metal cross tucked into a limestone cliff. The man-made structure stood out of place amid the majesty of nature. As the boat drew closer, they could see a wide concrete dock, and farther back, a Soviet-era block building that jarred against the wooden buildings they'd seen in El Nido. They motored past it. Jemma wanted to ask why, wanted to tell the man she was pretty sure this was where they needed to go...but she chose to stare at the water, afraid to sound stupid or draw any of his attention.

Mr. Lucky looped the *Baby Roxanne* around and pointed them at a crescent of white beach. He pushed the canoe toward the shore and cut the engine. The boat drifted until the low bottom scraped on the sand.

"You'll forgive me," he said. "I'll drop you off, then take the boat out to sea. I do not like this place."

Jemma barely listened. She considered the land...postcard-perfect beach, framed with tall, jagged cliffs and brilliant palm trees. A dark path led between two towers of rock into the jungle. Framed with gray stone, a Virgin Mary statue rested in a dark grotto. The sun hung low in the sky, and cast the beach in shadow.

"Ready?" Alex asked.

Though she was too hot by far, sweating through her clothes, she had to pause and admit the island was beautiful.

"Ready," she said. She helped herself down the boat's rickety ladder, and hoisted her skirts to slog to the beach. She could hear Alex behind her. She worried about jellyfish and stinging things as she walked.

She stopped. The island carried an aura of stillness.

"Can you feel that?" she asked.

"No," Alex said, stepping onto the beach. He carried his flip-flops in his hand...what would they do if something stung him?

Dried seaweed and exotic shells littered the beach. The seaweed lay in arcs, perfect impressions of the shape of the waves. Lucky poled the boat back into open water. The only sounds were cicadas and waves, the occasional call of a bird. After the blasting motor of the *Baby Roxanne* and the thick gasoline and fish smells, the island seemed so clean and quiet.

Intense peace washed over her. She'd felt some unpleasant places in her time—the English castle and an Italian restaurant in Lower Manhattan were two of the worst, but this place reminded her more of a desert. Empty. A sanctuary. Her mind wandered, unbidden, to a dark suburban basement and she closed her eyes. She let the island tug the bad thoughts away.

"What's he doing out there?" Alex asked.

She stood up, brushed the sand from her skirts and squinted out at the *Baby Roxanne*. "Fishing?"

"No...but he sure seems antsy."

Jemma shrugged. In her journal, Rebecca wrote about how much she loved the island, and after a little while here Jemma knew she would too. No wonder they'd considered this island a spiritual place.

"How does it feel to you?"

Alex always claimed not to be sensitive. He played poker well: he could discern a person's tells within minutes of meeting them, and could map out their exact agenda. Like Terry's dead wife. When she talked to him about it, he only ever smiled, looked at his shoes, and insisted he was merely observant. He watched for things, nothing more. It still helped to ask him what he felt.

"It's all right."

"Just all right?"

"Yeah. A little weird."

"What's weird about it?"

"For one thing, I'm a New Yorker, and I can't hear another human being. I've never heard quiet like this in my life. Freaking me out. And..." He grappled for the right word. "And it seems like a dark place. You said a girl burned herself to death here in front of a boatload of Japanese tourists. I have a hard time imagining the spirits here to be cheerful ones."

Alex headed toward the Virgin Mary statue. In her outstretched hands she held a giant clamshell. It looked clean enough to eat from...not even sand filled it. Two more shells sat at the lady's feet, but were filled with refuse from a hundred tropical storms.

Mary herself stood peaceful, her downcast marble eyes fixed on the white shell in her hands, her lips pursed in a solemn, pious frown. The unremarkable statue huddled protected from the elements by a dark little cave.

They moved on toward a dark jungle path and the air around them turned cool as they moved into the shade. Jemma hovered at Alex's back and let the lack of sensations wash over her. She wanted to go first, she did. But this was easier.

They came out of the jungle into a clearing, a big court-yard of sorts for the dormitory. A marble gazebo stood over the Virgin Mary. The statue was identical to the one on the beach, save for the absence of the giant clamshell. This Mary's out-stretched hands were empty. Cool and inviting benches beck-oned from the shade.

"This marble is from the same place as the Taj Mahal," she told Alex. He ran a hand over one of the pillars.

The gazebo's curved roof reflected a blast of white light from the sun. Jemma averted her eyes. Even behind her sunglasses, the light hurt.

Alex went off to explore, to see if he could get into the dor-mitory. Jemma lowered herself onto the cool marble of one of the benches and admired the lovely grotto.

Spirits are sometimes shy, and she hoped sitting quietly might bring some to her. More likely their equipment would pick some up overnight. She couldn't wait to see what the read-ings found. But that was a project for tomorrow.

Alex moved from window to window, peering inside the blocky building. The sounds of the island lulled her, soothed her. So much so that the cacophony of *Baby Roxanne*'s engine starting, moments after they'd left the beach, startled a small cry out of her.

Alex sprinted past her, down the little jungle path toward the beach.

"Hey! *Hey!*"

Jemma smiled a little smile. Mr. Lucky was taking the boat back to El Nido. She and Alex were alone on this island.

Once Alex ran out of sight, Jemma tried to remember a time when she'd been outdoors and not able to see another person. She remembered a time when she was indoors and very alone. That time she pushed away, tamping it down.

She supposed she ought to go to Alex. She stood, stretched in the sun, and followed the path he took to the beach.

The white sand lay in disarray. He'd run back and forth, and now he stood panting, wet and covered in sand. The distasteful sound of the *Baby Roxanne* faded into nothing as the little boat rounded a spit of land and vanished from sight.

"Easy," she told him.

"How can you be so calm?"

"We're in paradise."

"We're on an island that drives people to kill themselves. We're trapped here. And it makes you act weird."

"I'm not acting weird. I'm not panicking. It's a beautiful place. You can't argue."

"You're right. It's lovely. That said, I'd like a way off it."

Alex seemed afraid. He scanned the jungle. Nothing here would harm them, she could feel it.

"I thought about bringing a satellite phone, you know?"

She began to tune him out. "I'm sure we'll be rescued."

He gawked at her.

"What?" she asked. Terry knew where they were. Besides, this jungle must be full of things a person could eat.

"I hope he makes it quick."

Jemma frowned. He didn't like her happy. Why did he hold it against her that she liked this place?

Alex stalked off down the beach, kicking at the sand. Jemma drew deep breaths of fresh air. She couldn't see the downsides that upset Alex. She hated people; it was her dream to be this alone.

He came back after a few moments.

"Okay. We sit tight for a while. Hang out. Relax. Once we have our shit together—or I have my shit together, as you seem unmoved by the fact that we're marooned—we have to find water. Food can wait, water's the first priority."

Jemma watched the sea.

Alex flopped onto the sand. The breeze blew it around, and Jemma could feel it in her teeth. Not ideal, but it didn't ruin the loveliness of the vista. She folded herself in, and sat beside him.

Six

The sound of a boat out on the water brought Terry to the beach. The *Baby Roxanne* approached, teal hull bouncing over the waves. This was early. Too early. Mr. Lucky rode in his boat alone.

A million scenarios darted through Terry's head. He glanced up at the sun. It wasn't even noon yet, hours of daylight remained.

As long as she hides, she should be safe.

Terry jogged into the shallow sea and waded over to where Mr. Lucky moored his boat.

"Where are they?" he called.

"I took them to the island."

"But *where are they?*"

Mr. Lucky hopped into the shin-deep water with a splash.

"I took care of them."

"You killed them?" Terry lowered his voice. Relief flooded him, like a cooler of Gatorade poured over a winning coach.

"I left them. She'll take care of it for us."

The relief left as quickly as it arrived. For a moment Terry's thudding pulse overcame the rest of his world. Then it receded. "No. We don't know what they brought. What they know. They could kill her."

Mr. Lucky stared at him with the least expressive eyes Terry'd ever seen.

"All I care is that they don't write this book."

"If they kill her, they'll write the goddamn book." They couldn't kill her. He wouldn't stand for it. If they'd come all this way to write the book, they must know her weaknesses, her vulnerabilities.

"Did they carry a *bagacay*?" He racked his brain to remember if he saw them carrying a sharpened spear. "Did they smell like garlic?"

"Doesn't matter. If they kill her, they starve on the island before they can write a thing." Mr. Lucky made to walk past him, and Terry stuck his hand out to stop the bigger man.

"No," he protested.

Mr. Lucky pushed Terry's hand away and slogged toward the shore. Terry stood in calf-deep water, thinking. He had to go out there, to make sure no harm came to Virginia. He wanted to cry. No one paid Mr. Lucky to think; he simply did what he was told. Dammit. Terry hated this helpless feeling, the one he'd felt so frequently over the past four years. Virginia and the people of El Nido played him like a pawn.

He had to go to her. Couldn't simply leave her there. His boat, the *Virginia*, was indisposed, taking three French tourists and a South African on the C tour. He glanced at the *Baby Roxanne*. What would Mr. Lucky do? What could Mr. Lucky do to him?

Mr. Lucky made it to the beach and paused to talk to a little Filipino boy. The boy played with a discarded plastic cup, using it to mold shapes in the sand. He smiled up at Mr. Lucky as he passed. Probably a nephew or cousin. Everyone was related to everyone here. Everyone kept a nose firmly planted in everyone else's business.

Terry made up his mind and hauled himself up and into the *Baby Roxanne*. He poled out into deeper water, got the boat turned around, and fired up the motor. Mr. Lucky ran after him, even plunged into the water and swam a few feet, but the *Baby Roxanne* left him behind. Mr. Lucky gave up, slapping the water with his broad palm and cursing in Tagalog. Terry pretended not to hear. He would save his wife, and no one could stop him.

Seven

Alex didn't want to go into the shadows. He didn't like this place, and it blew his fucking mind that Jemma seemed so taken by it. Suicides don't make for nice environments. He wasn't sensitive, but did believe there were things out there he couldn't see. The equipment would take interesting readings when they set it up tomorrow.

If they made it back...

Why would Mr. Lucky have left them here otherwise?

The jungle teemed with life. Alex wondered how many creatures out there watched him as he blundered around. He'd hoped to see monkeys and monitor lizards. Now he didn't want to see either.

They had to kill time somehow. He steeled himself to explore. To do exactly what they'd set out to do. While he walked the path, he thought about Ralph's signal fire. Was Jemma his Jack? Or was Jemma Ralph, and he was Piggy?

Alex stared into the jungle, at greens so dark they turned black.

"I haven't sensed anything," Jemma said.

"No?" With all the surrounding creepiness, he expected a maelstrom of spirits.

"I'm rather sad about it, actually. Though they may be shy, they may only come out at night. I'll know for sure after we set our gear up."

"Or night falls on the island here."

"I would be surprised if we spent a night here and didn't discover some evidence of the supernatural. I'd rather not be here when that happens."

So she didn't entirely adore this place. Though he felt petty, it pleased him. Made him feel like they played on the same team again.

"I'm thirsty," she said.

He agreed, and listened as hard as he could. The wind in the trees mimicked the sound of water rushing over rocks. He wished all this nature would shut up. Give him the sound of horns, of cars, shouting. Good, city, human sounds. You couldn't be isolated in New York.

"Maybe that's a path?" She pointed to a black spot of jungle, darker than the foliage surrounding it. "It could lead to water? Maybe the stream that runs red?"

Before he could argue, before he could tell her the gaping mouth scared the shit out of him, she headed off. He wasn't particularly interested in finding a blood stream, particularly when they'd been abandoned here.

The trail reminded him less of a trail and more of a route frequented by hungry predators, the vegetation worn down by wily, ravenous paws.

"I hear water," Jemma said. He willed her not to be so loud here. The jungle bore down around them, listened to each word.

She froze. Scanned the trees.

"Something's here," she said. He'd heard the expression about blood running cold, but there in the jungle he felt it.

"Hello?" she cried. He first resisted the urge to pounce on her and clamp a hand over her mouth, second the urge to bolt back to the beach and wait it out. A boat would go by at some point, surely?

"Hello?" a voice echoed back.

Jemma and Alex stared at each other. Someone else on the island. Someone else who spoke English.

Alex still wasn't sure they should answer. Just because they called "hello" didn't mean they were friendly.

"Hello!" Jemma called back. She moved past him, and he reflexively shrank out of her way and gave her space to pass unimpeded. "We're coming!"

Alex could have kissed Terry he was so happy to see him. The perpetually nervous Englishman stood by the dormitory.

"Are you all right?" He stared past them at the jungle, his brow furrowed. *Oh shit, what was back there?* Alex kept looking over his shoulder, trying to figure what kept Terry's attention.

"We're fine," Jemma said.

"What the hell happened to Mr. Lucky?"

"Mr. Lucky has had a family emergency." Terry scrutinized the vegetation behind them. He turned and headed to the beach at a brisk pace. "He asked me if I would be so kind as to see to your safe return."

"He left us here without a word!" Jemma said.

Terry kept glancing over his shoulder, past Alex. Every time, Alex looked back, too.

"The island's a nice place," Jemma said.

"I'm so glad you like it. Let's get back to the resort now." Alex could have kicked her as Jemma said: "Already?"

"We've had plenty of time to check the place out," Alex said.

"What did you find?" Terry finally focused some attention on Alex. "No, never mind, we can talk on the way back. Get on the boat, please."

They waded out to where the *Baby Roxanne* bobbed in shallow water. Alex never thought he'd be happy to see that boat. Once they were on board, Terry flipped the ladder up, and shoved out to deeper water. He kept looking back.

He's scared.

"Sorry to be in such a hurry." He started the earsplitting motor. He fingered his wedding band and glanced back at the island. "Tell me, please. What did you find?"

"Nothing. It's a pleasant, lovely place. Why doesn't anyone go there anymore?" Jemma gazed up at him earnestly. She shouted to be heard over the roar of the motor.

"You know about the suicides?"

"And that means no one visits?" It didn't add up to Alex. He thought of the suicide forest in Japan—that didn't keep people from visiting. It became a popular tourist destination.

Terry stole another glance at the island. "The natives are a superstitious bunch."

Jemma said, "But it's not only natives around here...the

tourists might enjoy the place. And they would have no idea about the suicides."

"Is there something there we should be worried about? You seem kinda nervous."

Terry licked his lips. "Just getting a headache is all. I don't much care for these gasoline fumes."

"Will Mr. Lucky bring us back to the island tomorrow?"

Alex wished Jemma weren't quite so anxious to go back.

"I'm sure he would be happy to. As I said before, he's had a bit of a family emergency, and is very sorry for the inconvenience."

Look me in the eye and say that, thought Alex.

The ride back didn't feel as long as the morning's ride. A brisk wind picked up behind them over the open water. Jemma got splashed by a large wave. After that she withdrew, shivering. Her black clothes held the damp, chilling her.

"We'll be back in time for a hot shower," Alex reminded her.

"Thank heaven for small miracles," she said. Her good mood from the island waned. Alex's mood switched inversely.

Back at Vista Breeze, Terry killed the motor and poled the *Baby Roxanne* in to shallower water. On the beach, looming like a small mountain, glowered Mr. Lucky.

"I see he's back from his emergency."

"I'm sure he took care of it." Terry focused on setting the boat right. "*Baby Roxanne*'s his livelihood, so I know he's anxious to see her back."

They plodded to shore. Jemma hauled her soggy skirts around her and scowled.

"I'm going to take a shower and a nap," she said. Alex wanted to advise her about not napping, but rather powering through the jet lag. He held his tongue. "Let's meet at six for dinner?"

Mr. Lucky stood as they passed.

"Everything all right?" Alex stopped to talk with him. Jemma kept going.

"Fine, thank you."

Mr. Lucky's words were polite, but his body language screamed rage. His fists were balled, his shoulders tense. He glared at Terry and his boat. How long had Mr. Lucky waited for *Baby Roxanne* to come back?

Alex decided to drop it, to soak up some sun on the beach. He moved as far as he could get from Mr. Lucky and still eavesdrop, pulled the towel from his bag, and laid it out on the warm sand.

A scream.

Everyone on the beach—Alex, Mr. Lucky, a smattering of tourists and Filipinos—froze and turned toward the resort.

Jemma's scream.

Damn, who touched her?

Alex took off running. So did Terry, which saved him from a confrontation with Mr. Lucky.

Jemma sobbed in front of the little porch of her cabin.

"What happened?" He instinctively opened his arms to hold her.

She pulled back. "What are you thinking?" she snapped. "My door."

My door? The words didn't even compute. And she was right, what had he been thinking? He usually remembered to keep his hands to himself.

"I'm sorry," he said.

"It's on my door!"

Alex diverted his attention to her door.

"Jesus!"

Terry appeared behind him and made a little strangled gasp.

At first he didn't understand what he saw. Maroon paint? A tiny fur coat? No…an animal. Roadkill on her door?

He took a step closer and recognized a white patch of fur, still clean amid the carnage.

One of the bearcats hung there, nailed into the wood, next to Jemma's lucky number six.

Eight

Once again, Mr. Lucky pulled the *Baby Roxanne* up onto the beach at Sakripisiyuhin Island's natural cove. His chest hurt from the anger. He should be at home this night, eating his wife's dinner, playing with his son. It was dark. It was late.

He wanted to turn his back on Terry Brenton and walk away from his mess. The *Aswang* had always been a part of the island, but since the tourists stopped going there, it became more work to keep it away from the city. Terry worried the *Kanos* would kill the *Aswang*? If they could kill it without it infecting another, maybe they would be rid of the thing forever. He wondered what his father would say about that, or his grandfather. They'd protected the island and the *Aswang*, too. These days were more complicated than back then.

Now he brought it alms. People on the island upset it. It would be hungry and if someone didn't tend to it, it would hunt.

Mr. Lucky nudged a huddled form on the bottom of the boat. It mumbled, whimpered, cried out in a language Mr. Lucky didn't understand. JapaChineeKorean something or other. He couldn't find anyone willing to come tonight. It was too soon after the last alms...people remembered. Then he found this Chinese boy—or whatever he was—puking in the alley behind a bar, right handy to the *Baby Roxanne*. Slinking through the shadows, Mr. Lucky watched the boy and nailed him on the back of the head with the butt of his .45. The kid pitched forward and landed face-first in a puddle of his own booze-stinking vomit. Mr. Lucky slid one arm around his neck, the other behind the knees, cradling the boy, carrying him back to the boat, being none too gentle as he made his way up the steps.

Now, here on the island, Mr. Lucky shoved the prone form off the bow of the canoe. The kid splashed into the shallow water, then came awake with a yell, and flailing arms and legs. He spattered the calm seas with drops of water. Mr. Lucky liked the willing ones. They never started screaming until he poled out of their reach.

The kid tried to climb up onto the boat, but Mr. Lucky rapped at his knuckles with a long bamboo pole. He used it to push the boat out into deeper water, happy to leave the kid behind.

Feng sucked in a mouthful of warm saltwater and struggled to maneuver himself upright and out of the water. His hands and knees scraped coral, and finally his head broke the surface. He inhaled, thankful for the fresh, clean air. A boat. He reached for it, trying to figure where he was, why he was in the water, and why his head pounded. He tried to get his bearings. Darkness draped everything like a blanket. He caught hold of painted wood with one hand, and reached up with the other, but before he could pull himself up, a brown face appeared over the edge and whacked at his knuckles with a long pole.

Skin split and Feng cried out, splashing back on his ass in rocks, coral and sand. The man poled the boat away from shore, and Feng sat, too stupefied to try and follow. The last thing he remembered he'd been drinking with his buddies. He'd needed to throw up, but he must have passed out in the process, and now he was...here?

The boat's engine rumbled through the night as it started. Feng called out, first in Mandarin, then in English. "Come back! Help me!" But no help came from the man on the little boat.

He turned to the dark shore behind him. A white strip of sand separated dark jungle from dark sea. A jellyfish brushed against his calf and he yelped, then started to cry.

What the fuck happened? Happy and drunk one moment, fucking marooned the next. Could he cut through the jungle and get back to town? He paused and listened, but heard nothing except night noises: waves lapping at the shore, leaves rustling in a soft breeze. Feng dragged himself out of the water, and fished his expensive cell phone out of his pocket. Ruined, most likely. Maybe it had one more call...maybe he could phone for help? Something? Anything?

No dice. The big screen stayed dark.

Feng dropped the ruined smartphone in the sand. Maybe he'd been punk'd. Maybe this was a reality show.

He called out: "Hello! You got me! You can come out now!" Only the soft jungle sounds responded. He tried again in English, then sat next to his phone and listened to the trees and the water.

Not quite sober, he started to doze off.

"Hello? Is someone here?"

Feng scrambled to his feet. A woman. Holy shit.

"Hello! Over here!" She spoke in English, so he did, too.

He could see her clearly because she wore white. A flowing dress hugged her curves in the breeze. The most beautiful woman he'd ever seen, and Chinese, too! He asked, in Mandarin, if she spoke the language, and she told him she did.

"Do you have a phone?"

She moved close enough that he could see her delicate features. Exquisite lips begged to be kissed. An adorable little nose. But her eyes...what was wrong with her eyes? Funny contact lenses? Why did she smell like rotten meat? She changed, then, from Chinese to Caucasian, her hair transitioning from silky black to light brown, and her body type shifted. Her nose and lips transformed. Feng broke to run, but didn't get far.

Those were Feng's last thoughts as the woman unfurled leathery white wings. Her jaw dropped like a snake's, revealing a too-wide mouth of cruel teeth. She took the top of Feng's head off with her first bite, cruel teeth crushing through bone. Red blood spattered her white dress. She sank to her knees with him and began to feed.

Nine

Jemma holed up in Alex's cabin for the afternoon, which left him awkwardly displaced while Terry and Anna worked to get the dead bearcat off Jemma's door. He'd hung around at first, offering to help, but Terry snapped at him. He'd had tears in his eyes. Alex couldn't tell if it were compassion for the animal, embarrassment, or both. He swung past the bearcat cage and found the male—Alex couldn't remember his name but remembered it had something to do with Popcorn—pacing and agitated.

"Don't blame you, little buddy," Alex said. Popcorn blinked up at him with red-brown eyes. "I wish you could tell me who did this to your girlfriend."

Close to six Alex headed back to his cabin. They still needed to eat, they'd missed lunch. He knocked on his door. Jemma stalked out past him, went to her cabin and closed the freshly scrubbed door.

The next day, Terry couldn't find anyone willing to take them to the island, no matter how much money they offered. Alex hung out on the beach with his book for a while. He lingered by Jemma's cabin around lunchtime, but seeing the door closed and the blinds drawn, he decided to head into town without her in search of food. Despite the sights and sounds of paradise, he had trouble getting into the paradise mindset.

When dinnertime rolled around, he went to Jemma's door, hoping he didn't have to drag her—metaphorically of course—to eat.

She opened the door in reasonably good spirits. Weird. "Shall we go to dinner?"

"That's the plan. Are you okay?"

"I'm all right. Sad about the bearcat. Angry we've lost a day of research. But you know what this means, right?"

"Someone around here thinks killing animals is awesome?"

"No, we're on the right track."

Alex stayed silent, waited for her to continue.

"We were abandoned on the island, and now we've got this warning on our door. On my door."

They trudged up a path to the main road and flagged down a trike. Alex sat facing back, letting Jemma have the larger seat next to the driver. Alex handed him twenty pesos, and they were off, hurtling down the rutted dirt road, past bamboo buildings toward El Nido. Western standards of cleanliness did not apply here...half-stray dogs and cats sauntered through restaurants, flies landed where they pleased.

The small, bustling city of El Nido only comprised a few blocks, but it was vibrant and full of life and color. Alex liked it better now that Jemma was with him. Most things felt better with Jemma, especially when she was happy. Myriad smells permeated the air—all the seafood one could imagine, pork adobo, curries, scents from a bakery. Underneath it all floated an undertone of less appetizing scents—sewage, unwashed bodies, gasoline.

Alex led them to a cozy bar and grill that specialized in seafood. Their table sat on the beach, plastic legs dug into the sand, and it looked out over lots of little boats like *Baby Roxanne*.

"It's called a *Bangka*," Jemma said.

"What?"

"Those canoes. They're called *Bangkas*."

They ate in silence for a bit. Alex ordered a pizza, which didn't taste at all like pizza in New York. Jemma ordered fish *kinilaw*, a ceviche-type salad.

"Should we go back?" he asked.

"Yes, once we finish."

"No, I mean back to New York. Have we bitten off more than we can chew?"

As it grew dark, she'd taken her sunglasses off, and now studied him from across the table. "We don't even know what we're dealing with here yet."

"We're dealing with something someone is willing to kill over."

"We weren't going to die on the island."

"I'm not talking about that. Some sicko sacrificed an animal and nailed its carcass to your door."

"Are you afraid?"

He found it hard to answer. He didn't see things or feel things the way she did, but he knew they'd had their worst day of ghost hunting yet. This had always been something of a game to him. Fun. He'd read a meter and make extrapolations. They'd revealed a decades-old murder in England, and talked to girls who'd killed themselves because of a lecherous pedophiliac headmaster in Connecticut. He didn't see ghosts, hear voices, feel chills.

"I want to be sure you're safe."

"So far so good." Her weak smile didn't convince him. She chewed on her lip a bit. "I'm not sure what we're dealing with is even a ghost."

"What else could it be?"

"A demon? I don't know. I'd like to set up my instruments tomorrow, let them run overnight, analyze the readings, and then we should plan on an overnight."

"And you think that's a good idea?"

"How else will we know?"

A brash waitress cleared their plates while shouting something in Tagalog to a friend of hers down the beach. They paid the check. Alex chuckled at how fucking cheap everything here was.

"Let's hit a bar."

"Must we?"

"What better way to get a feel for the place?"

"Perhaps you should go...I can go back and work on the diary, the power's on so I can do some more research online."

"It would be fun...a drink? Loosen up?"

"No, not tonight."

"You want me to take you back?"

"I'm all right. I'm not a child."

He wanted to open his mouth, remind her of the dead

bearcat nailed to her door. But she was right. She wasn't a child. He offered, she declined.

"Are you going to go back to your cabin?" Alex asked. He didn't like the idea of her being there alone.

He studied her. He never knew how far to push or when to let her go. Would her strange attire make her more or less of a target? He walked her to a trike, paid her way, told the driver where to take her. He wondered if he'd done the right thing as he went back to the bar. Wondered if he'd ever see her again...

Alex ordered a frozen piña colada and wandered over to watch the lights reflecting off the water.

"Excuse me?" An American voice, and not a vapid-sounding one.

Alex turned. The woman's short, no-nonsense brown hair framed her face in a way that might be adorable, he couldn't tell yet. Her eyes were big and brown, and she looked very young. He could tell she wasn't, though, from the way she carried herself, and the more conservative cut of her clothes. Her T-shirt and capri pants were almost matronly by the standards of the bar.

"Is this seat taken?" She pointed to the plastic chair next to him.

"It is now. Please, sit."

"I'm Karen Heath." She stuck out a warm, dry hand, calloused from work. They shook. Alex introduced himself.

They danced through the customary "where are you from" conversation, he from New York, she from Minnesota. He discovered she worked for an NGO, trying to teach self-employed tour guides how they could conduct their business better for the tourists and better for the environment. She neared the end of her year here, and didn't know where she might go next. Inevitably, she asked, "What do you do?"

Alex had a lot of fun with this question. "I'm a research assistant on a book," he said.

"About what?"

"Hauntings. For this book, I've been to a haunted forest in Alaska, a school in Connecticut, a castle in England, and now a haunted island here on Palawan."

"A haunted island? Where? Is that the one with the shrine?"

"Yeah, out past Helicopter Island."

"Have you seen ghosts there?"

"Not yet. We got in yesterday. Today we went out for a few hours…"

"The morning doesn't seem a very good time to see ghosts."

"It's not. That's why we did it. Wanted to get a lay of the land without any distractions." Alex couldn't help thinking of being left there, and little dead bearcat eyes.

"We used to have a ghost in our house." She leaned in as though she were confessing to killing a man.

"Yeah?" Everyone had their own ghost story. It was a great way to pick up chicks.

"A ghost cat. We didn't have a cat, but all sorts of catlike things happened, stuff fell off high shelves, you know the sound when a cat startles and runs away really fast?"

Alex could think of a handful of nonspectral reasons for this, from small earthquakes to a rat infestation, but he held his tongue.

"Tell me more about the El Nido ghost," she said.

"You know…it's not super pleasant. I'd rather not." Alex didn't mean to pique her curiosity; he honestly didn't want to talk about it. He expected her to press him, but instead she simply sat back on her bar stool, and changed the subject.

A Chinese woman, maybe twenty, appeared at the bar between them. She spoke in deliberate, heavily accented English. "Have you seen my brother Feng? He is Chinese, he is maybe eighteen? He wear a red shirt. I lost him last night."

They both said they hadn't seen him, and apologized. The girl frowned. "Sometimes he drink too much. Thank you."

The woman made her rounds, and Alex noticed a lot of head shaking. No sign of Feng. Finally the woman had some luck a couple of bikini-wearing blondes, one of whom pointed toward the door, then shrugged. The woman nodded, gave a slight bow, then followed the girl's finger.

He and Karen kept chatting. She was nice…but off. He couldn't put his finger on it yet. He debated needling her, getting her talking about herself, but decided he might like to get to know her in a more honest way. It started to get late, and his thoughts strayed more and more to Jemma.

"Um," Karen asked shyly, "where are you staying?"

Alex grinned. "Vista Breeze," he said. She smiled at him, then reached out and took his hand. She squeezed it.

Wow. Human contact. Alex tended to forget how much he missed it until he felt it.

"Are you going back to the island tomorrow?" Karen asked.

"I hope so...we're having some trouble with our boatman."

"Well that's no good. Tomorrow's my day off. I'll take you guys out if you want."

"Nah, we'll make do." He didn't want to impose. Or endanger her. Though a little voice reminded him the biggest danger they faced yesterday was being stranded.

"I'm out on the islands all day every day. I know my way around. Even a haunted one." She smiled, a clean, neat smile. Alex liked it.

"It's too much to ask," he said. "Especially on your day off."

"Don't worry about it. It'll be fun. And I get to meet Jenna."

"Jemma," Alex corrected. She did that on purpose. He could tell from the way her lips moved. She liked him and she was jealous. Sweet. "It might be dangerous."

"I carry a pistol. In case I run into any pirates, or anything I can't otherwise handle. I've never had to use it, but it might make you feel better to have it along."

Karen wasn't afraid of the island, and she lived here. Maybe he was being stupid. Maybe they were onto something.

"Okay. What time's good for you?"

"Whenever you want to go."

"It's your day off."

"Is nine too late?"

"Let's say ten."

On their way out, they saw a crude missing-person poster stapled to a wall, the text in three languages. A smiling girl, blonde hair, Marissa Mulchahey, last seen on the twenty-third.

Ten

Karen arrived on the beach at ten as she promised, wearing shorts over a conservative one piece black bathing suit. Alex admired her cleavage as she dragged her little motorboat ashore under ominous gray skies. He did a double take when he read the name: *Lucky Daze*.

Karen thrust out a hand to Jemma, who kept her arms folded over her chest, gloved hands tucked into her armpits. "I don't touch people."

"Sorry." Karen turned the shake into an awkward wave. Alex went through introductions, and Jemma turned to tend to their gear. Her mouth made a straight line as they loaded cases into the boat. Jemma picked up the ectometer's waterproof Pelican case. She left the heavy one with the microphones for Alex. She slogged out to the boat, ignoring the water that soaked her skirt. They brought nine microphones, which would be placed in various locations on the island and picked up the next day.

The waterproof gear, made for outdoor use, could be set up as usual, even in the inevitable rain. Karen used a long pole to push them out to deeper water before starting the engine. Alex drank in her exposed, tan skin, the way her curves and muscles worked together for a complete picture. It made a contrast to Jemma, who sat in sullen, sodden black.

Waves splashed up over the sides of the *Lucky Daze*, soaking their feet and the bottom few inches of Jemma's dress. She dropped her head into her hands. He could tell she didn't like his choice of a new boatman.

"Are you feeling okay?"

Her glare was daggers, a melodramatic shake of the head "no," then she dropped her head into her hands. The choppiness of the water made his own stomach start to rebel, too. But he knew Jemma's issues went deeper than an upset tummy.

Instead of motoring to the serene beach where Mr. Lucky had taken them, Karen tied up her boat at the concrete dock on the other side of the island.

"I thought it would keep your skirts drier," Karen said.

"Won't much matter when it rains." Jemma helped herself out of the boat. She could at least *try* to be nicer to Karen.

The island was a different place in the dreary gray light. The rain muted the green of the palms, and birds didn't cry out to welcome them. Alex's intuition rankled: this was a bad idea. A bad, stupid, awful idea.

Karen peered up at the sky. "It'll pass. It will pour for a half hour, maybe, then blow by." She headed down a little path, leaving Jemma and Alex to set up the first motion detectors on the dock.

Jemma aligned the height on the tripod and angled the microphone to pick up the greatest spread of noise. She kept her eyes on her work, sulky.

"This is still better than Mr. Lucky." Alex punctuated with a smile, hoping to cheer her.

She ignored him. "I want to put the others by the gazebo, and near the doors of the building. Where else do you think? We've got another set."

"On the trail, maybe?"

"Okay. I want to go and take some photos. See if I can pick anything up." Jemma let her hair hang in her face, a mask between her and the world.

Was Jemma giving him time to hang out with Karen alone or was she pissed at him? He couldn't decide if that was kind of cool or totally not cool at all.

"What do you expect to find?" Alex set up one of the tripods, growing irritated at the tightness of the screw knob as he adjusted the height.

"Does it matter?"

Uh, yes it mattered. While he was technically only a

research assistant, he still would be doing a great deal of work on the chapter. He needed to know her thought process in order to properly calibrate the equipment. "I want an idea of what we think we're doing here."

"It's a site of violence and there's no spiritual activity. That's fucking weird."

Jemma rarely cursed. Alex waffled...push her or get away?

"But what do you think the mics are going to pick up? Or the cameras?"

"I don't know," she snapped. "Not everything is logical and laid out. Don't you get that? It's why we're here. Go see that Karen isn't messing anything up." Alex studied her. He hated when she lashed out like this, and in his experience, it was best to leave her be.

"Fine." Alex turned his back on Jemma. He hoped she'd be all right and carried one of the tripods onto the path. It didn't feel right leaving her alone, but he wasn't her babysitter.

The wind picked up, and the trees began to sway. The storm rolled across the water, an elegant, inevitable force of nature. Lighting flickered inside it. Leaves on the palm tree whipped back and forth in the wind. He stuck the tripods into the soft dirt as hard as he could and snapped the waterproof casings shut. He found Karen on a bench near the back of the dorm, a view of the dock and the *Lucky Daze*, an e-reader in her hand.

"Storm's rolling in across the water."

"Where's Jemma? We should get inside, wait it out in here." Karen tucked the e-reader into her bag

Alex considered the dormitory building. In bright sunlight it stood foreboding, blocky, and ugly. In this gloom it resembled something from a nightmare.

Karen regarded the sky.

Alex debated going for Jemma. She'd seen the storm just as clearly as he had, and headed off into the jungle anyway. It would only piss her off if he chased after her. He debated for another beat. "Let's go."

"Should we get Jemma? I don't think she likes me."

"Jemma doesn't like anyone. She went out to get some

pictures, she'll come in when she's ready." It felt like a betrayal to say out loud, but it was all true.

Karen led the way. They shielded themselves as best they could from the rain. A moment before they got inside, the skies opened up. Sheets of water dropped from above, and palms swayed and bent in the wind. Where the fuck was Jemma? He shouted her name, but the wind stole his voice.

"She knows where to go."

Karen was right, of course, but Alex couldn't help thinking about Jemma's irrational fondness for this island. Would it cloud her judgment? What if a tree fell on her? What if she got scared?

Karen pulled a big LED flashlight out of her pack once they stepped inside the cold, dark dormitory. "Have you been in here?"

"Not yet."

"Now's the time for serious exploration. What do ghost hunters look for?"

"Anything out of place, anything that tells us about people."

"What do ghosts look like?"

"I've never seen one."

"You're kidding."

"Never."

"Then why—"

"I've heard things, like on the mics we set up today. And I've seen pictures. Taken pictures. But never seen a ghost. Jemma sees them."

"Are you sure she's not messing with you?"

"Positive. I trust her with my life. With more than my life."

"Must be nice." The understatement of the century. He should go. Should go get her. But...maybe getting caught in the storm might make her more ready to leave. Make her willing to give it up.

"So let's explore," he said.

The first room used to be a bedroom. Three bunk bed frames sat pushed against a far wall. No remnants of inhabitants were here, no signs that posters or pictures once hung on the chipped stucco walls. Alex thought of how Jemma described the island in a spiritual sense—devoid of personality. This room was the same.

They moved on to the next room. Alex stuck close to Karen and her light. This was an excellent flirting opportunity—he knew that, Karen knew that. He wanted to...but he couldn't stop thinking of Jemma. Where was she? She had some common sense...why didn't she come in from the rain?

The next room held the same three bunk bed frames, though this time with the mattresses and pillows still on them. It stank with mildew.

They made their way up to the second floor and watched the storm for a few minutes. It wasn't like thunder storms in the city, that was for sure. Not like ones anywhere he'd ever been. Dramatic and dynamic, the rain pulverized the jungle.

"There's a basement," Karen said. "It's locked, but I've never tried to get in."

"If the door's wood, in this humidity, I can't imagine it taking much to get inside."

"I think there are records and things stored down there."

Jemma would like those. They should wait for her for some of this. Maybe she could...he didn't know. Sense some activity here.

"Tell me what you know about this place," Karen said as they headed back down the stairs to the basement door. Sand and leaves piled in the corners, but the path to the door was clear, almost as if someone other than themselves had trodden it recently. Icy fingers crept up his back. He asked himself why he kept putting himself in the path of this spooky shit.

"I know women lived here. Nuns watched over them, but it wasn't a convent. It was a spiritual retreat kind of place. You could come and stay as long as you wanted. It was expensive, I hear. Then girls started doing freaky things and killing themselves, and the place closed down. Used to be on the tourist circuit, too much unpleasantness happened, and they stopped."

"Freaky things?" Karen asked.

They arrived at the door. Alex pulled a bobby pin out of his pack and started to work on the lock. Again, he could use this as an opportunity to flirt. Some of Rebecca's diary was quite risqué. "Some of the ladies decided to try a little experimentation," he said. Something in the lock gave. "But the sister who set herself on fire in front of a big pack of tourists was the last straw."

"I read about that," Karen said.

The lock clicked, loud even against the backdrop of the storm. "It's open." Alex tugged at the door, and the swollen wood dragged against the tile floor. "Shine your light down here." Karen cast her light into the black maw of the basement. The dormitory was dark in the gloom of the storm, but the basement redefined dark, wooden stairs disappeared into nothing. Musty dampness flowed up to them.

"No, here." He pointed down, to the floor in front of the doorway. Karen did as he asked, and he could see scrapes in the floor, more than could be from his opening the door.

He tried to justify why someone would be using this door. And why it would be locked.

When Karen first turned on the flashlight, it seemed very bright, almost unnecessarily so. But shining down into those stygian depths...

"We're gonna need a bigger boat," Alex muttered.

Karen went first, because she carried the light. Alex hesitated. Where was Jemma? Karen and the light moved farther away, and, silently apologizing to Jemma, he headed down.

The stairs creaked, and he worried about his weight on the rotten wood. Need to give up the Twinkies.

The basement seemed carved out of the stone of the island. Karen flashed the light around the room to reveal three dark doorways. A warren of god knew what.

But then again, wasn't this what the thrill of being a ghost hunter was all about? Dark places, things that go bump in the night? It wasn't as fun without Jemma.

Alex touched the moist stone wall to steady himself, took a last look up at the gray doorway, and followed. He thought places like this weren't supposed to have basements. Wouldn't floods or earthquakes or high water tables or something make it a poor choice? He stood behind Karen—close, but not touching; he was very good at not touching—and peered in the room.

Old church robes, old churchy stuff, nothing personal, nothing meaty, nothing interesting. They moved on to the next doorway. Maybe Jemma would have been able to pick something out, but it looked stinky, musty, and boring to him.

"Oh, wow," Karen muttered.

"What is it?" He resisted the urge to take her shoulder and peer over her. She most likely wouldn't have minded, but he never touched anyone unless they asked for it. Not these days.

"Someone's been living down here."

When Alex's turn to peek came, he saw some of the mattresses from upstairs arranged into a neat little pile, with a few blankets folded on top of them. A few other personal items: a tarnished silver hairbrush, a sliver of a mirror. A picture of Donald Duck holding out flowers to Daisy hung on one wall.

"A woman," he said.

A sound from behind them made Alex jump and Karen cry out. Something blocked the gray light from the open doorway.

Whoever or whatever's den they'd stumbled into had arrived home. Where was Karen's gun?

A patch of lightning illuminated the stairwell. The creature on the stairs lurked dark and formless. Karen shrieked, but as the thing took a step, Alex recognized the gait. "Jemma?"

Karen shone her light in Jemma's face and she raised a gloved hand against the light.

"Are you alright?" Karen asked.

"Come down, check this out. Do you feel anything down here?"

"No, nothing. Just like the rest of the island."

Jemma scuffed down the stairs. She shivered, soaked, but Alex couldn't do anything to warm her.

Karen shone her light in the little room. It smelled like the rest of the basement, yes, but with a thicker, muskier smell. And underneath hovered a sweet perfume Alex didn't recognize.

"Can you feel anything here?"

"Nothing. If a person were living here I'd expect to be able to pick up something, but...nothing."

The final room yielded more surprises. A bloody sweatshirt with the Gap logo lay crumpled in the corner.

Jemma took a few steps forward, as if to pick it up, but Alex stopped her. "I wouldn't." He no longer wanted to be down here. He didn't want to be here when the inhabitant of this basement came home.

"I'm getting something faint from the sweatshirt—fear, confusion. It's only a thread, though. It'll be gone soon."

They trudged up the stairs, relief flooding Alex as they wert. The storm had stopped, and patches of blue peeked through the clouds.

"This will blow off soon. It's going to be beautiful later," Karen said. She resumed her spot near the dormitory's back door with her e-book while Alex and Jemma set up the rest of the tripods and microphones. He pulled the memory cards from the storm and stuck them in his pocket. It was unlikely they'd picked up anything other than the sound of rain and the leaves, but it didn't hurt to check it out. He went tripod to tripod and calibrated the sensitive machines to the sound of the trees. Anything else—bird call, thunder, heavy wind, would trigger them. Also any spiritual noises. Or human noises, for that matter. They took a winding path back to the beach where Mr. Lucky dropped them on the first day.

Eleven

Soaked to the skin, Jemma slogged along the back trail. Alex carried the remaining cases behind her on the path. She wanted to turn on him; ask him why he wasn't off with his new girlfriend.

Jemma saw something in the jungle during the rainstorm. A dark shape moving through the trees, something she wasn't meant to see. She didn't know what it had been, but the room in the dormitory made her think. They weren't alone on this island. She sucked in a deep breath of the clean air. No ghosts, no nothing. So empty. Peaceful. Maybe she hadn't seen a some-one. The being who'd been living in the basement had something to do with the aura of the island, she knew it. She'd never heard to of a ghost that didn't give off some kind of signals, though. That left no psychic fingerprints behind.

Jemma emerged from the jungle and onto the white beach, watched over by the Virgin Mary. The sun burst out from behind one of the last dark clouds and lit the beach with its warm glow. Jemma looked away from the glare of Mary's white marble. Up past the tidal line the sand looked disturbed. What kinds of animals lived on the island? What was big enough to disturb the sand like that? Could it be rain? Little pockmarks covered the sand, but the passing squall didn't have the energy to wipe out these scuff marks.

"There." Jemma pointed at the sand. "It looks like something was dragged down the path." She racked her brain... what animal lived on the island and could leave a trail like that? The big trail headed toward the gazebo. "There are monkeys," she said, "though I didn't think they lived this far north on the island. A monitor lizard?"

"Maybe a seal or something? A sea turtle? Are there even seals down here?"

They set the Pelican cases down out of the reach of the green, foamy waves. Jemma pulled her camera to her eye and started to snap pictures.

"You okay?" Jemma wished he would leave her alone. She knew she was being unpleasant, but jealousy and guilt and shame swirled within her, she knew it was irrational, but she couldn't stop it.

"I'm fine. I promise. Focus." She pointed the camera around at the island, taking photos. You never knew what would show up on a photo. Orbs, sometimes, though 99.99% of the time those were just dust. But the camera could catch things that the naked eye didn't. She hoped the rain hadn't damaged it.

Like that footprint. An unfamiliar sneaker, the print protected under a palm frond. She moved her face away from the viewfinder. Someone else had been here, that was all. *On her island. Trespassers.*

"I bet it's nothing," she said, her voice tight. She snapped more pictures. "What's Karen wear for shoes?"

"Boots. It's not nothing," Alex said.

Jemma took more photos. Maybe these were their footprints, from the day before yesterday. A handprint, but the smeared, pock-marked sand distorted its size. She leaned in close and focused her lens. Where the beach ended and the jungle began, the drag marks stopped, but in the jungle there were a few scuff marks. Red mud.

"Oh fuck." Alex pointed. She could just see his finger, huge in her zoomed lens. Palm fronds, dark red-brown with blood.

"We shouldn't go any further," she said. "Messing up evidence."

"You think the cops in this backwater are gonna be all CSI on this shit? What if it's the ghost, teasing?"

Jemma stared at the blood through the camera. It could be. Ghosts did do this kind of thing. But it didn't *feel* like spectral activity. It felt like *nothing*, which meant it had to be real. She pulled the machine from her face and looked at the blood spot.

Moved closer. She closed her eyes, tried to let whatever the island had to offer wash over her.

She felt the slightest tropical breeze. The sun peered through the passing clouds of the storm. Birds and bugs made a symphony, complemented by the waves lapping at the sandy beach. Nothing out of the ordinary. At least not until she opened her eyes and saw the blood again. Maybe it wasn't blood. Maybe it was from the rain.

Alex popped open the second case and pulled out the ectometer. It took a few moments to assemble the device, and it made a science-fiction whirring sound as it charged up. Alex ran the meter over the blood spots. The needle never moved.

"You've got the camera, you go first."

She hesitated.

"Sorry, babe. We can trade..."

No. She wanted the camera. It made her feel safe. On leaden legs, she headed down the trail.

"This meter's giving me nothing," Alex said, from behind her. Of course not. Because there were no ghosts on Sacrifice Island. Something else lurked here. She knew it. She'd joked about a demon the night before. Today it wasn't funny. Did demons live in basements? Did they covet GAP sweatshirts and Daisy Duck?

The trail to Mary's gazebo didn't yield any more information. Jemma photographed roots and leaves and the sky, a big wasp with a white face, and a black-and-white bird.

Lovely white benches surrounded Mary in a peaceful ring. The birds still sang. The corner of one bench, protected from the afternoon rain, was smeared with rusty dry blood. Jemma paused, taking pictures in high resolution. She turned the camera on Alex and saw him through the viewfinder. Alex waved his wand.

"There's nothing. We have to find Karen and call the police. Stop fucking around." Jemma's feet weren't listening, though, and she pressed onward. Under the sound of the birds, the sound of the waves lapping at the white beach, she could hear another sound. Buzzing.

She didn't want to see the source of the blood, human or

animal. She knew it was human. The smell hit her then—something rotten and dead.

She stepped past Alex, fixed on the screen. It felt more like fiction when she saw it on the tiny screen. A dried chocolate syrup blemish on the smooth, perfect marble.

Her sandals scuffed loudly on the sandy marble.

"Oh," she said unconsciously. Her view screen showed her a hand, bloated from a day in the heat. Alex abandoned the smear he'd been metering and came to her side. Captivated, she clicked the shutter.

"This is Feng. His sister was looking for him at the bar last night."

Feng became pixelated and small through the camera's screen. Click, click, click. She could see and not see, all at the same time.

He didn't look like a person anymore. He lay curled up on the floor in front of the Virgin Mary, protected from the rain. His body had been thrown against her and fallen at her feet. Feng's Airwalks were clumped with sand; his unharmed legs were clad in stylishly tight jeans. Blood, dried to look like chocolate, spotted his T-shirt.

She photographed a bit of black hair, and a horrified brown eye with an epicanthic fold. The left side of the boy's head was gone, his skull a messy, jagged crater. *Head wounds bleed a lot.* She couldn't stop taking pictures.

"Jem, enough," Alex said behind her. She couldn't stop, though. She documented every angle of the kill. The moment she stopped she had to check in with reality. Click, click, click.

"Come on. Put it down."

She whimpered.

Alex reached out and pulled the camera down, careful not to touch her white fingers. She took one more crazy shot, depicting sand and lines of motion, and Alex's shoe.

"Maybe a rock crushed his head," Alex said. She turned to the dark windows of the dormitory. They both knew it wasn't a rock that crushed Feng's head.

It appeared something, something with a sizable maw—lion or baboon, something big, had taken a single bite of the boy's head, it crunched through skull and obliterated nose, eye, ear, and the whole back of the skull. The brain seemed notably absent.

"Ghosts don't do this," Jemma said.

"It's like a zombie movie."

Jemma kept her eyes everywhere but on what they'd found.

"What's that?" Alex pointed at some new horror.

Jemma flinched, her muscles tightening, as she prepared for the hungry beast to appear.

"Come look."

No no no! But she went. Alex pointed to Feng's biceps. Though they were swollen from the heat, she could see a clear bruise. A handprint. As though someone with small, strong hands took Feng by the upper arms. Shaking him. Reprimanding him?

Or holding him to bite off his head.

"Must be pre-mortem."

She agreed. "It wouldn't have bruised otherwise."

"Maybe the sister? Bitching at him? And that's why he ran off?"

Jemma raised the camera and snapped a few more photos, focusing on Feng's bronze-colored arms.

"Maybe," Alex said. He leaned in close. "Let's get out of here. No point in putting up any more audio gear. Cops will trigger it. I gotta find Karen. Head back to the boat."

As she walked back to the dock, Jemma swapped the camera's memory card with an empty one. Jemma watched the patchy sun on the water from the concrete next to the *Lucky Daze*. She heard Karen and Alex before she saw them. Karen sounded scared. Good.

They boarded the motorboat, and Karen turned over the engine, startling a flock of black birds from a tree.

The sound of the motor and the roaring of the wind made conversation on the trip back to the resort impossible. Jemma fingered the memory card in her pocket, thinking about what she'd seen, and what it meant.

Karen deposited them in hip-deep water. She apologized and told Alex she'd see him later. She waved good-bye to Jemma and motored off. They slogged to shore with the gear they hadn't set up. Jemma's soaking skirt clung to her body. Karen had probably never seen violence like that before. Jemma felt worldly and wise. Panting, they plopped onto the cases in the sand.

"That's not a ghost," Jemma said, out of Karen's earshot.

"No shit. I'll get the tickets squared away, we can be back in New York by dinner tomorrow."

"No!" Jemma whirled on him. "We can't go."

Alex stared at her.

"Something killed him. I want to know what. And we've left our gear on the island."

"To hell with the gear. Did you see that kid? Something tore off half his face. I don't want that to happen to," Alex paused, and Jemma felt 90% sure he would say *you*, but instead he said "us."

"There's a killer out there, and if we mess around, he could get us."

"He or it?"

"He."

"Or she?" Jemma remembered the smell of the perfume in the basement. "How can you be so sure?" she asked. It hadn't left anything behind, a human killer would have left passion, or joy, or anger...something. The air surrounding the Chinese boy tasted stale and flat, like a glass of water left on the nightstand overnight. It tasted like nothing.

"It was the same person who put the bearcat on your door."

He was right. A nervous person. She'd been able to taste that when she went back to her room and opened her sparkling clean door in the dark.

"You're back?" Terry's ever-enthusiastic, always-too-loud voice shook them from their thoughts.

"We are," Alex said.

"We need the police."

Terry's eyes went wide. Jemma turned to Alex, who watched him.

"There was a murder on the island."

Twelve

Terry drove them in the cheery green and white Vista Breeze van to the El Nido police station. Alex couldn't get what he'd seen out of his head—it brought about a newfound respect for soldiers and doctors and people whose professions regularly brought them in contact with savaged flesh. After baking in the tropical sun all day, the van's vinyl seats seemed ready to sear skin. Alex pushed himself not to think about what this heat continued to do to Feng's body. Things decomposed fast in the jungle. He let Jemma sit up front—he was never sure if he should, was it still the gentlemanly thing to do when she wouldn't speak a word to the driver? He didn't know, but felt like a dick perching in the front seat and chatting it up with Terry while she sat alone in the back.

On this ride, however, no one spoke.

The El Nido police station didn't resemble an American police station in the least. One whole wall stood open, a neatly dressed officer sat outside at a picnic table with a woman in a hijab. He didn't get up when they came in.

Alex watched as he made eye contact with Terry, and noticed the slightest dip of the officer's chin. A greeting? No, it didn't feel like that. It felt like an affirmation. Of what?

They sat at a second picnic table. Rich wood made up the station floor, peppered in sand. Palms shaded them from the sun and made for a cozy grotto. Outside on the street, two boys kicked a soccer ball, so old the black had scuffed off most of the spots. Every so often one would glace at Terry. They gave him little knowing smirks, and Terry would turn away.

Jemma occupied the smallest amount of bench she possibly

could, her hands folded in her lap. She sat with the general air that she didn't deserve to take up furniture. Alex often tried to imagine her reclining or sprawling and could never do it. At present she seemed ready to bolt and flee.

Minutes chugged past. The woman tossed her head back and laughed. She touched the officer's arm. Not flirting, a familiarity suggesting complete comfort. A sister? A cousin?

"What's taking so long?" Alex kept his voice low.

"He'll come over when he's ready." Terry continued, seeing Alex's exasperation with his answer. "The pace of life is slower here."

"Wouldn't the pace be faster if he knew someone was violently killed?"

"I'm not even sure the island is his jurisdiction."

Sometimes America seemed an imperfect hassle, but the legal system and the predictability of home seemed infinitely far away.

Two uniformed high school girls walked by, saw Terry at the police station, and started chattering among themselves. Coincidence, Alex told himself. But coincidences, like mermaids and unicorns, were made up.

He glanced at Jemma, trying to see if she picked up on the fishy weirdness.

One of the soccer boys shouted something at Terry.

"Do you speak Tagalog?" Alex asked.

"Never learned. My wife took a class, but I never did."

"How long have you lived here?" he asked.

"Fifteen years."

Alex liked to think if he gave fifteen years of his life to a place that wasn't home, he'd at least pick up some of the language.

The officer stood, gave a great stretch, shook his friend's hand warmly in both of his, then sauntered over to them. He sat on the bench next to Jemma. She pulled away as discreetly as possible.

"Mr. Brenton. What may I do for you this afternoon? Are your guests having trouble?"

"These are the researchers here to study Sakripisiyuhin Island."

The officer's demeanor changed. He stood straighter, and the corners of his mouth, which had been turned up in a smile, sank into a flat line.

Jemma seemed to notice this, too, and scooted a fraction of an inch away from him.

"Welcome to El Nido," he said, no warmth in his voice. "I hope you are enjoying your stay here."

It seemed wise to let Terry do the talking.

"They were on the island, and they ran into some trouble." The flat line of the officer's mouth dropped into a frown. "That is to say, they found some unpleasantness, and reported it back to me, and I was most unhappy for them to have seen what they saw—"

"We discovered a Chinese boy who'd been savagely murdered," Jemma said.

In the moment before the officer put on a surprised expression, his shoulders drooped and his eyes dropped. Then he seemed to pull himself together. "My goodness, I hope you were not hurt, were not upset! Let me accommodate you for one of your nights with Mr. Brenton for free so you will not think poorly of our people."

Free hotel room? A man was dead.

"Where did you find this terrible thing?"

"On the island, in the marble gazebo," Jemma said.

The officer nodded. "Well, we will go and take care of it. Thank you for your time." The officer stood, pulled a radio out of his belt, keyed it, and spoke in Tagalog.

Terry stood up, but Jemma and Alex stayed put. The officer seemed surprised to find them there when he finished the radio call. He listened as someone else spoke.

"Come along," Terry said.

"But don't they want to know what we found?"

"They will go and see for themselves."

"But we could have—" Jemma let her protests trail off midsentence. "Do they not care?"

"Of course they care!"

"Was it because I said he was Chinese?"

"Things work differently here. The pace of life is slow. The detectives here don't follow the same procedures as home, they don't have the money or the training to conduct what you and I might think of as a real investigation."

"There's a violent murderer here," Jemma said. "And all those missing people!"

"I'm sure most of your missing people are relaxing on a beach miles and miles from here, and the worst culprit is poor communication." Terry favored them with a grandfatherly smile.

"If you don't mind, I think we'll stay in town for a bit."

"Can I recommend one of the massage parlors?" Terry asked.

"Sure." Alex let him point one out and talk about how fantastic the service is.

"It's a real massage—not anything unsavory like you might read about in Thailand."

"Thanks, Terry," Alex said. He breathed a sigh of relief when the man's white-shirted, sweaty back faced them as he returned to the van.

Thirteen

"What's wrong with him?" Jemma couldn't fathom that level of not-caring. "What's wrong with all of them? How could no one care?"

Alex nodded in agreement. "It's bullshit." He took a deep breath. "Which is why we've got to get out of here? Like tomorrow. This is way over our heads."

They walked down the streets of El Nido. Early afternoon sun scorched the city, and the streets were the emptiest they'd seen. Jemma baked under her hat and in her dress, sweat pooling on the small of her back and between her breasts. They passed scores of shops that sold a variety of things: dresses, cheap packaged junk food with Chinese labels, poorly painted and brightly colored toys.

"Go?" No. Impossible. They didn't even know what precisely they were dealing with. Didn't this excite him? And what about Rebecca? What if her spirit were still somewhere on the island? "We can't go, Alex. We only just got here."

"I've seen enough dead stuff. There's a bagel shop in Yonkers. A poltergeist. It's perfect, and close to home."

"The book is about the world."

"New York is like the center of the world…"

"I miss it. But I want to know, don't you? What kind of spirit tortured Rebecca in her journal? Who killed the boy? Who's living in the basement of the dormitory?"

"Who wants us gone so badly they nailed an animal to your door?"

"They don't feel the same way about animals here as we do."

"All the more reason to leave."

"One more day."

"One more? Are you kidding?"

"Let's at least see what the gear has recorded." She couldn't bear the idea of leaving.

At a concession stand, Alex bought them each a bottle of water.

"I don't know. It's dangerous."

"We solved the murder in Canada. We proved the Eskimo fellow did it."

"I'm pretty sure they prefer to be called Inuits. And I agree. That was awesome, it felt really good. But this isn't the same. That murder happened almost a decade ago. We're stumbling across bodies and shit here."

"We'll get more media attention, and more publicity, and then grants will be easier to come across."

"Not if we're dead."

They wouldn't be dead. They'd have an even greater knowledge of the spiritual world. Not that Alex cared. She tried not to be mad, but this was vacation for him. This was work, exploration, for her.

They found a restaurant on the shore, with tables set up in the sand. As the tide receded, it left exotic shells and trash in its wake. The Vista Breeze beach was much cleaner, and there were fewer boats moored there. She was glad Terry caught them and talked them into staying. She liked being away from the sounds of the bustling city.

Terry. She needed to talk to him. To find what he knew about the island. What he wasn't telling them. With his information, they would be much better prepared for their next visit.

"I'm calling tonight to get tickets home squared away."

"I'm not going," she said.

"You're kidding. I don't want to do this. Not here. It's not right. This isn't our kind of case."

"I don't care. It *is* our kind of case. We thrive on the unexplained."

"What if I leave?" Alex asked.

He wouldn't go if she stayed. She knew he wouldn't. "Fine. Leave."

He stared at her. She could almost see his mind race, reaching for an answer. He opened his mouth, closed it.

"You're being a bitch." He stood up, gently pushed his chair in, and walked away.

Jemma stayed in her chair. The waitress came and Jemma panicked, ordered a mango shake. Did she have any money? Did she have anything? She searched her deep pocket and came out with a dirty, soft bill. She did have enough. She paid the woman when she brought the icy drink.

Jemma liked the island. Liked the quiet, the idea that everyone who died there, even Feng, had moved on. No one was trapped in a purgatory. She had to find out why.

Alex wouldn't leave.

What would she do if he did?

It didn't matter, because he wouldn't. End of story.

For a half hour, Jemma debated whether to walk or to use one of the trike taxis to get back. All she had to do was raise a hand to flag it, say the words "Vista Breeze." Just like she had the other evening. Which went all right. But what if the driver didn't understand. What if it were awkward? What if he did take her, but then they went in a different direction? What if he were confused? Or worse…what if he took her somewhere else?

She started to walk back, but then realized it was too hot. She had to flag a trike down after all.

None of them stopped and she started to cry. Finally one pulled to the side of the road. It took three tries to spit out the name of the place.

"You okay, lady?" the driver asked, his English broken.

"Fine, thank you." She turned away. The made herself small in the little cab of the trike. She could smell the driver's cologne. He tried to talk to her over his shoulder, taking his eyes off the road. Her one-word answers dissuaded him and he gave up. The rest of the ride was in silence. She stumbled out of the cab, recoiling when he tried to offer a hand to steady him. She practically threw the fare at him, trying to organize her skirts so she wouldn't trip. She knew she'd overpaid, but she didn't care.

Relief washed over her as she retreated to her cabin, shut the door behind her, locked it. She drew all the curtains, and only then did she step out of her layers of clothes. What would it be like on one of those deserted beaches? What would it be like to swim?

It didn't matter. She stepped into the shower and soaped herself up. The icy water soothed her after her ordeal.

Alex couldn't go. She needed him here. She'd have to go to him and apologize. Tell him she needed him. But she wouldn't go. She touched her skin. It didn't hurt when she touched herself.

She remembered, dimly, what it felt like to be touched.

The cold water sluiced over her until it became unbearable and her teeth chattered. She shut the water off and toweled dry. She put on a dress, hating it for being shapeless and ugly. But it was who she'd become, an embodiment of ugly shapelessness. It was her lot in life to be alone, deserted even by Alex, her closest friend.

She donned a hat and stepped into the baking sun. She started to sweat again. She imagined her New York apartment, curling into a chair with her work, a blanket wrapped around her. A mosquito whined in her ear and she swatted it away.

Alex wasn't in his cabin. She found him instead at the beach with a paperback, watching two little boys throw jellyfish at each other. They laughed and splashed, squealing when the stinging masses would land on their bare skin. Her hatred of humanity welled up inside. Boys torturing each other and innocent creatures.

"I'm sorry," said Alex.

At least he apologized. "I'm sorry, too," she said, to be polite. "So you're not going?"

"I wouldn't leave you, you know that."

"You scared me."

"I know. I'm sorry I got mad."

"We can't leave. What if we find why the ghosts don't stay here and can bring peace to other ghosts?"

"This is way out of our league."

She knew she'd won.

"Think of the press we'll get. This could be some serious money for us. Thank you, Alex, I know you're making the right decision." She sat with him for a bit, but watching the boys play became too much. Jemma drifted off. She would find Terry. Get some answers out of him. She came across him upstairs in the restaurant where he stood with an empty glass in his hand and gazed out at the sea.

"Can I buy you a drink?" she asked.

Terry chuckled. "I own the bar. There's no need. Would you like something?"

"Bottled water, please." Jemma didn't drink. She couldn't let her guard down.

They sat at one of the Molave tables. A lizard basked on the railing in the sun.

"You said your wife had a connection to Sacrifice Island."

"I'd rather not talk about it."

Jemma frowned and gazed down into the bottle of water. "It would help our research. I don't want any details, anything unpleasant. Whatever you could tell me would be helpful."

Terry peered at her a moment. Jemma wished Alex were here, wished he could tell her what might be going on under Terry's surface.

"You should leave."

"I love it here," Jemma lied. "I don't want to leave." A mosquito whined in her ear. The heat of the afternoon made her sweat without even moving.

"Do you really love it here?"

She smiled because he'd seen through her. "I do like the island. There's something about it, it's peaceful in ways that I've never seen before." Terry gave her a tiny half smile. She went on: "It's the only place I've ever found where I can really hear myself think. Where I can relax and be myself."

"Does Alex agree with you?" Terry asked.

Jemma felt he knew the answer to that already. "No. He doesn't like it. He thinks it's frightening."

Terry nodded. Then he sighed. "My wife lived there. In the early nineties."

Jemma did the math. The island closed down in 1994 after

Rebecca and three other girls killed themselves. "Did she know Rebecca St. Germaine?"

"How do you know that name?" Terry set his fresh drink down on the table. He looked scared.

"I have her journal. It's what brought us here."

"She left a journal?"

"Yes, I have it in my cabin."

"I haven't thought of Ms. St. Germaine in a long time."

"Can you tell me anything about her?"

"Like what?"

"I only have her journal, where it seems as though she's going mad. What was she like? Was she close to your wife?"

"My wife's name is Virginia. Virginia Weston, back then. They weren't especially close, but they both spent a long time on the island, so they knew each other. They were friends. Rebecca seemed pleasant enough. But she was in pain all the time, and never let anyone get close to her."

"Her diary describes an affliction, but she never says what kind."

"He—her husband—destroyed her left hand." Jemma thought of the lovely script from the diary, and imagined what she would do if she lost her hand. Lucky Rebecca that he didn't take her dominant hand. "I'm not sure how much you know about her."

"Please tell me," Jemma said.

"She married young. She was seventeen, her husband thirty-four. She was British—titled, after the marriage. Lady St. Germaine. But she wouldn't hear of her title being used. He died in a hunting accident. Virginia always said she hoped Rebecca killed him. He did awful things to her, and because of it, she wouldn't trust anyone."

Jemma knew the feeling well. Understood it.

"He crushed her hand when she disobeyed him."

Jemma wanted to know how he'd done it. Specifics. But she only nodded.

"None of it healed right. Left her with a mangled claw. She kept it covered, it made her extremely self-conscious. Who can blame her?"

Jemma thought about the mangled hand, never mentioned in the diary. If one carried a physical token of torture, people wouldn't assume one was better simply because time had passed. The pain never went away. In a way, Jemma envied Rebecca's twisted claw.

"Did she like the island?" Jemma knew the answer to this after reading the diary. But she wanted to hear what Terry had to say.

"Loved it. Said she'd finally come home. In a way, I'm glad she died there, though I wish it had been under better circumstances."

"How did she die? I know she killed herself..." Jemma also knew she hadn't been part of the self-immolations.

"She died from blood loss."

"She slit her wrists?"

"Not precisely. Her throat."

"Do you have any pictures of her?" Jemma built an image of the woman in her mind as she read the diary, influenced by Daphne Du Marier's novel. Long brown hair, glowing smile, a mangled hand and none of the fictional character's confidence. But she did have her own kind of self-assurance as she went through with suicide.

Terry sucked on the end of his mustache. "I do. Wait here and I'll get them."

Jemma settled into her wooden chair. When Terry came back, he scared off the basking lizard. It skittered soundlessly over the edge of the balcony.

He handed her a stack of three-and-a-half-by-five photographs, the corners curled from the humidity.

The first picture featured a classic beauty—yes, just as Jemma imagined! The fortysomething woman in the picture was still beautiful. Thick auburn hair, lovely tanned skin. Jemma studied her. The smile shone too radiantly. And this woman clasped her hands in front of her. She flirted with the photographer.

This wasn't her.

Terry seemed to read her thoughts, and pointed to the background. Caught by accident, she saw a short blonde woman, with glasses and thinning hair. She wore all black, shapeless garments, and black cloth covered her left hand. Not beautiful at all.

"She looks so sad. How long did she live on the island?"

Terry took a moment to answer. "Three years."

"This is Virginia, then?"

Terry nodded. In all the pictures, Rebecca appeared as an afterthought, Virginia the main subject.

"May I ask what happened to Virginia?"

Terry picked up one of the photos. Studied his late wife. He set his jaw. "In 2007 she was diagnosed with cancer. It started in her ovaries—we were never able to have children—and by the time they caught it, it had spread. In 2008 she was gone." Terry collected his photographs. "Thank you for listening. I have to get some work done." He cleared his throat. "I think—I think you'd better leave. Go back to New York."

"What? I thought you wanted us to write the book?"

"I changed my mind. Go now, while you still have the option."

And Terry shuffled away.

Jemma smiled. The headmaster at the Connecticut school warned them off days before they learned he'd sexually assaulted five girls in his care. It meant they were close.

Fourteen

Terry always seemed to forget Mr. Lucky's massive size until he stood next to him. Terry found him in the late afternoon, hauling the day's catch of fish off the *Baby Roxanne*. Not enough to sell, but enough to feed his family.

"What do you want?"

"I wanted to let you know I talked with the woman. With Ms. Labasan."

"I don't care. I don't want to talk about any of them. You understand?"

"But she's not all bad—"

"She is exploring the island. She is going to find your wife. She's going to write a book about her. And everyone will know about the *Aswang*."

"Maybe..." Terry let his voice fade away. Maybe what? Maybe Jemma wouldn't find the secret they harbored on the island? Maybe she wouldn't write the book after all? Not bloody likely.

"And every time they go out there? She smells it. She gets hungry. And if I don't keep her fed, she comes here, to the town. And you know what she likes to eat."

Terry nodded, but Mr. Lucky went on.

"Sabu's wife is pregnant. I won't risk it. I have to find something to feed her tonight."

"I'll send them away," Terry said.

Mr. Lucky shook his head.

"Then they go to White Sands resort next door. Or rent a room in El Nido."

"We won't take them to the island. No one on the island will rent them a boat."

Mr. Lucky nodded. "Maybe. Maybe if we don't take them, and we tell the people in town not to rent them any of the boats."

"We'll try it."

"If they go to the island again, I will kill them." Mr. Lucky paused to light up a cigarette. The last fish in the bucket stopped flopping and splashing. "Karen told me they found where she sleeps."

"God."

"I mean it. I will kill them. I should bring them to her tonight, and then we be done with it. Let it go back to the simple ways. My father talks about what things were like as a boy, back before the tourists ever came. The *Aswang* ate well when the war was on."

"See to it she eats well tonight. Tomorrow I want to talk to her."

"No." Mr. Lucky picked up the fish and headed inland.

"I'll take my own damn boat if you won't take me."

"You go tomorrow I have to go back and feed her again."

"I'll bring her a dog."

Mr. Lucky's laugh rumbled. "She don't like dogs. You know that."

Goddammit. Mr. Lucky was right about everything. He didn't want to send them to their deaths. By a set of irrational double standards, the deaths of two people he'd met bothered him more than Mr. Lucky collecting drunken tourists and taking them to the island.

"Will you find someone at the bar tonight?"

Mr. Lucky stopped and shook his head. "Paulo's grandmother is very sick. We'd agreed she would be the next tribute, but I didn't think it would be so soon."

"Why not take—"

"Leave me to it. This is my job I must do. Karen will watch the man."

"Alex. His name is Alex."

"Mr. Brenton. I do not give a damn what their names are. To me? They are only food for our monster."

"She isn't a monster," Terry said weakly.

"You can lie to yourself all you want."

Mr. Lucky left Terry alone on the beach. He started to wish he'd never come here, but reminded himself he met Virginia on this island. A silver lining to everything. He loved her. They'd had so many great years together. Nothing could change that, no matter what she'd become.

He'd apologize sincerely and tell them he could not find a boatman to take them to the island tomorrow. Mr. Lucky would put the word out tonight; Terry would telephone Karen and make sure she knew. No more trips to the island.

They'd find a way, though. He ran a hand through his thinning hair, and plodded back to his resort on sand as white and fine as flour.

Fifteen

"Why didn't you go with her?" Jemma asked. Karen had called, asking them both out to dinner. Alex declined.

"I felt bad about yesterday. I wanted to hang out with you."

"I'm not going to be hanging out. I want to examine these pictures and do some writing."

Alex sighed. "You could hang out."

"I'm not here to enjoy the beach."

Alex decided to push forward. He needed her to let him know he meant something to her.

"Can I check out the pictures with you?"

"Fine," Jemma said.

The water sparkled in the sun, and everything smelled crisp and clean. Jemma turned and took the camera to her cabin.

Alex offered to open the windows since they didn't have power in the stifling room, but Jemma declined. He suggested they go up to the restaurant, which had a nice cross breeze.

"It's not dark enough for the pictures."

They both sat on the bed, with plenty of space between them. Jemma set the camera down and pulled the memory card out. Alex gave her the three from the recorders as well.

Alex picked up the camera and water ran out of it. Fucking hell, what was he doing here, other than throwing the University of Oregon's money away? If he didn't need to replace the lenses, he could maybe replace the body of the camera for seven hundred bucks. While Jemma loaded the pictures on her laptop, he carefully took the whole thing apart and set the pieces out to dry. At least it wasn't saltwater.

She turned the screen so they both could see. A lot of

green and a lot of gray crowded the images. She paused on each image, scanning for anything out of the ordinary. Orbs were usually dust—though pouring rain would cut down on the dust particles. She didn't use a flash, because the light reflecting off raindrops would create false orbs. It wasn't cold enough and no one was smoking, so any ectoplasm pictures would most likely be real. No funnel-shaped vortices, no dark shadows. That Jemma potentially killed the expensive camera almost made him want to cry. The whole trip made him want to cry. He scrutinized the faux-thatched ceiling (real thatch work and air conditioning don't go together) and heard Jemma suck in her breath.

"Right there," she said. It took Alex a half second to register and shake off his melancholy.

Jemma jabbed a gloved finger at the screen.

"Look!"

Something moved through the rainy jungle, captured in white. *That's not a ghost.* "Is that whoever's living in the basement?"

Jemma blew the image up until it became grainy.

"I think it's a ghost."

Alex leaned in. "I don't know. Looks solid to me."

He could barely make out a white form in the shitty image. The curve of the hip and buttocks appeared feminine. Foliage blocked the head and face.

"I wonder what our mics will pick up." Jemma frowned.

Alex racked his brain. He'd read a lot on the topic of paranormal investigation, and fancied himself pretty good at it.

"Could this woman be the reason we're not sensing any activity?"

Jemma thought for a moment. "Maybe."

"We need to find her. Need to let her know we're not going to hurt her. We just want to interview her."

"I have to research this. Dammit, when will the power come on? Is there anywhere we can go with Internet and electricity?"

"Soon."

Only twenty minutes.

Jemma stood up and paced. "I need to think on this. Thank you."

Dismissing him. He wanted to ask if he could stay. He hesitated.

"Call Karen back. Go to dinner with her," Jemma said. She pronounced Karen's name like a racial slur.

Alex flip-flopped in his mind. He could do that. He could do just that. And would probably have a better afternoon for it. He chewed on his lip for a moment.

"I gotta talk to you," he said.

"We're not leaving."

"No. We're not leaving, not yet anyway. But I gotta...you're acting jealous of Karen."

"Why wouldn't I be? You're all over her. You can't stop talking about her."

"No, I—"

"Fine. It doesn't matter. I have to figure out how the woman on the island is keeping ghosts."

"Or maybe she sends them on."

"Or whatever."

"Listen to me a minute, okay?"

She sighed, a dramatic heave.

"You're treating me like shit."

"You can do whatever you want with your free time. You're my research assistant."

"I want to spend my free time with you."

"Let's not talk about this, okay?"

"No, not okay."

"We can't possibly be together. You know it. I know it. So go fuck another floozy."

"I think we can, though."

Jemma laughed. A harsh, brittle laugh. "I won't put you through that. You've felt it. You can't touch me."

"I have a theory..."

"I know your theory."

"I honestly think it would get better over time. You touch me, I get your pain, then I touch you, and you get it all...I think if we touched long enough, it would reach an equilibrium."

"And you want to find out?"

"I'm willing to, yes. There's no reason you should carry your burden alone."

"Go be with someone you can touch."

"I want to be with you."

"No you don't. You only think you do."

"Don't tell me I don't know what I want. I make decisions for me."

"And I make them for me. And I want nothing to do with this."

"Don't be crazy…I love you—"

"I have no idea why," she spat, and tore off one of her gloves. She took three steps across the room and touched his face.

He had felt it before. All of Jemma's pain flooded into him. She was a wobbly vessel…if she touched someone with more pain than she carried, she would take it on. Someone with less pain, her pain seeped away.

Memories flooded him. Self-loathing. How did she live with this darkness? He saw John's face, remembered being stripped naked and tied to a table, raped and punched. Until she got a foot free. He lived the experience—not for the first time—as she kicked her husband in the face. And killed him.

Alex lived the energy pouring from Jemma—everything awful that John's abuse bottled up in her sluiced from her and destroyed her tormenter.

She has to let it go.

He knew he was right even as the fear she'd endured for four days before he'd rescued her consumed him. He relived the humiliation as he saw her, bound and naked and emaciated on the table.

It became a loop as he touched her in the memory and learned the whole story from her body.

The initial shock of her memories passed and left him sensitive and disoriented.

"I'm sorry it happened to you," he croaked. "But you have to move forward."

"Move forward?"

"Touch me. Right now."

They would pass it back and forth until it dissipated. He knew it.

"Get out."

"Take my hand, Jemma. Hold it. Don't let go."

"Get out!"

He went. Maybe he shouldn't have. Maybe he should have tackled her. Held her down and proved himself.

It wouldn't mean anything if it didn't come from her. If she didn't want it.

So he left, huffing a sigh, feeling flayed, raw and bitter.

Sixteen

The afternoon sun baked through Terry's light cotton shirt and linen trousers. Sweat pooled at the small of his back and inside his trousers. It was only Virginia. Nothing to be afraid of. Just his beloved wife. He'd had to wait a day, to make sure Mr. Lucky fed her, to make sure she wasn't hungry when he came. He arrived at noon, when the sun shone strongest and the creatures of the night were at their weakest.

Maybe she'd be asleep, and it would be a wasted trip. Mr. Lucky was angry with him, the ghost hunters were furious, asking him why they couldn't find a boatman. "The season is very busy," he told them, but they didn't buy it.

"Virginia," he said, in barely a whisper.

Normal jungle sounds answered him. How long could he justify staying here before he headed back to the boat? Back to Vista Breeze, where he would drink himself into a stupor. He'd lock himself in his cabin, close the shades, and fantasize about what would happen to Virginia and El Nido if he packed up and left.

"Hello, lover." Her voice was a liquid purr. It wasn't even her voice anymore…that's not what his Virginia sounded like. She'd been sixty when she came back to the island, when she came and never left, but the years melted away, and before him stood a woman in her twenties. He hadn't even known her when she'd been so young.

He reminded himself this wasn't her. Her true face was a horror.

She lingered in the shadows of the gazebo, avoiding direct sunlight. He stayed in it, let it blast him in the face. Maybe he would get cancer, he thought, willing it to be so. Any end would be better than this. He wished they'd realized that before Virginia made her choice.

The version of herself she presented wore clothes in a matronly cut. The thin material showcased her nipples, and tiny black panties through the skirt. She'd never had such a body, not even back before he met her.

If it's not her, then why stay? he argued with himself. *It is her, though.*

"You send me an old woman?"

"I'm sorry," he said.

"She was dying. I can tell. She was nothing. She was worse than nothing."

"You're going to be alone here for a while."

"They have to come collect their machinery." She pointed a long white finger toward one of the tripods. A blinking red LED greeted Terry's gaze.

He glanced up as he spoke, and saw her lips droop into a frown. She changed, body and clothes, before his eyes. She melted into forty-year-old Virginia, Ginny at her most beautiful, before the cancer. The clothes thickened.

"What will I eat?" she asked.

"We need to wait a bit. A week, maybe. You can go a week without food."

"I can't. You know I can't. You know it hurts when I'm hungry."

"Dogs then. I'll bring dogs."

"You'd have me eat dogs?"

"What can I do?" He wanted nothing more than to hold her, but when he'd tried, he found her cold and hard and nothing like the woman he remembered.

"I can't help it. I'm hungry. All these people here..." She pouted. "Feed me the ghost hunters. The woman smells delicious. She's miserable."

"They're here to write a book about the island. About you. What you do."

"You want them to kill me?"

Did they want to kill her? He didn't think so; he didn't know what they wanted. "What if she's the one?"

"You want to leave me again?" She gazed at him with Ginny's brown eyes. They almost melted his heart, but the whites were too yellow, and the rest too cloudy.

"You could rest." It's nearly impossible to kill an *Aswang*. But it could be done, the curse could easily be transferred to another. "Don't you want to rest?"

"You can't leave me," she said. "You'd be alone. You'd hate it."

"I would," he said, and he meant it. He couldn't imagine a final good-bye with Virginia, even after all they'd been through.

"I won't leave you." And he wouldn't. He wiped sweat from his brow. "No more food for at least a week. You used to go a month or more."

"I can't," she moaned. "You all smell so delicious. You intoxicate me. Your blood is warm."

"You can."

"You used to call me dear. Used to tell me you loved me."

"I have to go."

She took a step to the edge of the shadow, and held a hand up. The fingernails weren't right...they were claws, yellowish and curled.

He turned so she wouldn't see his tears and made his way back to Mr. Lucky's boat. Could Jemma be convinced to take her place? Could Virginia be convinced? He imaged Alex making the same decision he'd made.

"I miss you." Her voice was a salacious purr. "I'm lonely."

He broke into a jog.

Seventeen

Alex rarely took his shirt off in public, aware most folks didn't need to see his hairy, pasty, man boobs. But here the sun begged him to drink it in. His skin still tingled from the residue of Jemma's touch. Every follicle of hair seemed to ache. The warm water helped.

Jemma sat on the beach, a black-clothed sulking ball. They'd spent the previous day going from boatman to boatman, asking for a ride to the island. Each man looked longingly at the wad of cash Alex offered and said no. Alex called Karen in the evening, and she coolly told him they sometimes take a day to fish for their families.

The barking motor of the *Baby Roxanne* shattered his enjoyment of the afternoon. Alex paddled in toward the shore. Jemma looked up, away from her book.

Mr. Lucky helped Terry into the knee-deep water, and he waded ashore.

Alex splashed over.

"Have you heard anything from the police?" he asked, then paused. Terry's face was the color of cottage cheese. Red splotches stood out on his cheeks and the tip of his nose. His eyes were gray and watery.

"No."

He gazed past Alex, at Jemma. Fixated on her for a moment. Then he moved away from Alex, and headed to shore.

"Why are you upset?" Alex asked.

"Please, I'm in a hurry."

"I'll walk with you. What's up? Something upset you. Were you on the island?"

Terry stopped, wheeled around, and spat at Alex. "Please, leave me alone. This has been a most horrid day." He wheeled around and resumed his splashing stride toward the resort.

"Does this have to do with your wife?"

Terry wheeled again. "If you ask me another question, you and your friend will find yourselves out on the street. Do you understand me?"

That sounded like a yes. Alex waved to Jemma. He needed her help.

Terry stormed past her, up to the bar.

"You have to touch him," Alex said.

She stared at him for a moment.

"You must still be feeling pretty good from yesterday—" She flinched like he'd hit her.

"Fine. What do you hope to learn?"

"I don't know."

"Will I hurt him?"

"No. He's a mess. I wouldn't ask if I didn't think it would help."

Tears welled in Jemma's eyes. She wiped them away with the back of her gloved hand.

"You're sure?"

He was never sure. Could never be sure.

"I'm sure," he said.

She nodded, and started up the stairs. She peeled her gloves off as she went, and handed them to him, one by one, and dropped them into his hands, careful not to let her pale skin touch his again.

Terry picked up a bottle of rum from the bar. His eyes were red.

"Not now. I can't right now."

Jemma turned to Alex. There wasn't anyone else up here. Alex nodded to her.

He knew their skin brushing together could do it, but Jemma placed one hand on each of Terry's cheeks. Both of their eyes widened, Jemma's head flew back, and she began to moan, a lonely, agonized sound.

Eighteen

For a moment, Jemma felt her skin against Terry's. Touch. Skin. Another human. Twice in three days. A new record.

Then pain racked her. Tore through her, lighting every nerve on fire. She took his pain as it slammed though her, touched all of her, wave after wave of blinding white agony. She knew what it felt like to be a piece of driftwood, slammed against the rocks. Intellectually she knew she could handle this. She'd not often touched people who hurt worse than she did. Usually she hurt them, like she had Alex. But sometimes it went this way.

She let go when she slumped to the floor. But she'd seen it all—Terry's marriage, his wife's cancer, and the bargain he'd made. She saw his guilt every day, and his questions about what to do.

Terry extended a hand to help her up.

"Don't help her," Alex said. Red tinged everything...a burst blood vessel in her eye?

"Her nose is bleeding," Terry said. "What did she do?"

"She took your pain."

"I know...I feel...lighter."

"I need to get her to her room"—Terry reached for her hand again—"but we can't touch her skin." Alex lifted her into a chair. "Here are your gloves, sweetie."

He only talked to her like this when she lingered in this misty pain place, when she saw everything through gauze and haze and her body felt like she'd been used all over and in every pore.

She took the gloves. She had to put them on by herself. Unless she let him. He'd offered, after all.

She pulled them on.

"I need to lie down," she whispered.

"Gotta drink something first." Alex turned to Terry. "Orange juice? Something really sweet."

She drifted away for a moment and woke as Alex shook her shoulder. His touch—through her shirt—was brief and hesitant. "Here, we're almost done." Could she really have touch all the time if she let him?

The horrible juice, warm, thick, syrupy, and painfully sweet, dribbled down her chin. Her shoulder, tender from the pain, throbbed where Alex had touched her.

Old feelings flared: She wanted touch again, wanted a hug. At first she thought
keeping herself dressed, always covered, would help—but there had been accidents. It was easier to avoid everyone and everything. No one would want to touch her anyway. It was better, easier, simpler this way.

"Can you get up?" Alex asked.

Terry seemed to have gone, and they were alone in the restaurant.

"I don't know."

"We'll get you up, walk a little bit, and then you can sleep it off as long as you need to."

As if she were drunk, as if she'd done something bad.

But she was tired.

"Did you see anything?" he asked.

She nodded. "I saw everything." She couldn't organize it, though. Couldn't make sense of it yet. Needed to digest the images she'd seen—flashes of palm trees, starry skies, screams, hot winds, and a gaping loneliness that threatened to consume Terry, and now consume her. She needed sleep. Needed her body and mind to begin to sort what was Terry's and what was hers.

Nineteen

Alex closed the door on Jemma's cabin. Above his head fluffy white clouds punctuated the blue sky. He'd helped her get into bed as best he could, tried to make her comfortable. Now he would leave her alone, would...what? What the hell could he do? He walked to his own cabin, kicking at small stones. He wished she'd told him something, something to go on, start researching, get some balls rolling. Instead he could only wait, with the knowledge he'd caused his best friend pain. He hoped it wasn't as bad, considering she'd dumped all her bullshit on him the day before.

No. That wasn't fair. He'd done it to himself. And if he were really brave, once he had her back in her room, he would have touched her, and taken some of the pain himself. Doing what she asked seemed like a cop out.

He slid in through the cabin door, closed it behind him. No power. He took a moment to listen. Motorbikes and cars passed on the street, happy voices shouted in a language he didn't understand. Dogs barked outside. He couldn't help but feel responsible. The sensation churned in his gut. He wanted to go to her, take her in his arms, tell her he loved her. Console her. Make love to her.

An impossible dream. Always had been.

Prowling, he went out and paced in front of her cabin again. He scribbled her a note, said he was going into town, to use her cell phone despite the roaming charges and to call him if she needed anything.

Alex overpaid for a trike ride, got out at Louie's Backyard, and headed up the stairs. Soon he'd miss the sunset near Vista

Breeze. He didn't care. He didn't want a sunset. He wanted Jemma, but it would never, ever happen.

Alex ordered a drink from a brassy American woman. She introduced herself as the owner of the place, and he made half-hearted small talk. The overpriced drink made him feel better about overpaying the driver.

He took his drink out on the porch and gazed down at the crowded main street of El Nido. Tourists and locals swirled with trikes, scooters, and a rare pickup. Dogs, chickens, and cats threaded through them, weaving a tapestry of sound, motion, and color.

He thought about Jemma. About her affliction. He'd been the one to introduce her, at a college party, to the man who would become her husband. The man who would spend years mentally and physically beating her down as he descended into madness. Until finally he snapped. Alex hadn't seen the signs. Yeah, he knew his friends were withdrawing, but Jemma had a miscarriage. He didn't want to be pushy and intrude. He wished he had. God, he wished he had.

"Alex?" Karen stood in front of him. The setting sun kissed her tanned skin. Hunger for her swelled in him. No—not hunger for her. Hunger for a human. For anyone he could touch. Her short cropped hair, the neat bob, made him yearn to tangle his fingers in Jemma's thick black hair. What would it be like?

"Hey." He gestured for her to sit down.

"How's it going?" she asked.

"I've had a pretty god-awful day," he said.

"The island?"

"I wish," he said. "We still can't get out there. On top of that, Jemma ate something that disagreed with her. She's down for the count."

Should he not mention another woman? He told himself not to feel bad—Jemma had no interest in him (or in anyone, and probably never would ever again) and he was certainly free to have himself a grand old time. He checked his phone to be sure she hadn't called or texted.

"So I'm completely free for the night."

Alex watched her response, how she angled herself in the

chair toward him, pointed her feet at him, touched her face. All good signs. "Care to show me a good time? Show me around?"

"I can show you a good time." She smiled and showed off those fantastic white teeth.

Perfect.

She showed him a deserted beach on the far side of town, and he kissed her there as the sun went down. He brought her back to his room (she offered her place, but he wanted to be close to Jemma in case she needed anything). She told him she never did things like this, and he believed her. He told her the same thing, and didn't care if she believed him. He fucked her under the drone of the air conditioner, with the sound of a beetle hitting the overhead light, *tink, tink, tink*. She smelled like sunscreen, baby powder deodorant, and sweat. Alex imagined the smell of Jemma's shampoo. Imagined Jemma's breasts under his hands, imagined her calling him an amazing lover.

He silently thanked his lucky stars when Karen said she should go, she had to work early.

"I'll call you," he said. "Tomorrow, day after? We can grab a drink, dinner."

"I'd like that." Her good-bye kiss tasted like the mango they'd eaten, and made him smile as she left. He'd call her. He liked her.

Alex went to take a shower. He needed to cool off in the hot night. He soaped himself up and heard a knock on the door.

Jemma?

He barely rinsed, wrapped himself in a towel, ran to the door. Was she okay?

Terry stood before him when he threw open the wooden door. Dammit.

"I'll give you a moment to collect yourself."

Back in the shower, Alex finished rinsing, shrugged on a blue polo and a pair of khaki shorts. He opened the door and stepped out with Terry on the front porch. They each took a Molave chair.

"What did she do to me?"

Alex knew better than to play dumb.

"She took your pain. It'll come back, your memories are all intact, but she's given you a breather."

"Can she...see things?"

"She can see your pain. She'll know everything."

"Then I need both of you to come to the island with me tonight. I have to show you."

"Show me what?"

"She hasn't told you?"

Terry's sweat made a sour contrast to the perspiration Karen worked up earlier. He kept glancing around, unable to meet Alex's eyes.

"She's been under the weather all afternoon."

"I'm sorry to hear that, but I think she would find what I have to show you most interesting."

"I'm sure she would—I'm sure we both would. And tomorrow, when she's feeling up to it, we'll go."

"We have to go at night."

"Okay, tomorrow night."

"It must be tonight."

"No. Jemma can't be disturbed, and I won't go without her."

Terry stood to go.

"Wait up," Alex said. "What's this all about? What does it all have to do with the island?"

"You'll find out soon enough." Shaking—in anger? fear?—Terry talked off into the dusk.

Alex didn't want to admit Terry had freaked him out but he slept poorly, getting up over and over in the night and leaving his cabin. He went and stood in front of Jemma's cabin each time. And each time was the same. No lights on, not even the AC on. He wondered if he should knock. If he should try to get inside.

What if she needed help? What if she lay on her bed, unable to call for help?

Or he could be patient and respect her space.

Each time, he trudged back to his cabin, he cast glances over his shoulder. He wanted her to be all right.

And he wanted to know what she'd found out from Terry. Maybe he could be doing something instead of tossing, turning, and swatting at mosquitoes.

He eased into bed, drew the sheet to his chin, and stared at the ceiling.

Twenty

Jemma slept. And as she slept, she dreamed. She tossed and turned in her sleep. Sweat-soaked sheets tangled around her waist and legs. When she closed her eyes, she saw sharpened bamboo rods and black baby chicks.

She woke before the power went out and cast off the moist, stinking sheets. Her sensitive skin felt stretched, shiny, and new. Later today it would feel better enough to rub on some aloe lotion to soothe the pain.

It took hours to organize her thoughts. To weed out Terry's from her own, untangling them and tugging them apart.

There were no ghosts on Sacrifice Island. The lurking woman in white was much worse than any ghost. She'd experienced the moment when Terry met Virginia, when she lived in one of the rooms on the island and he was living in a room above a bar in El Nido. Jemma saw it all—each failed pregnancy, then Virginia's stomachaches, which were a symptom of a particularly aggressive cancer. Then she saw a much younger Mr. Lucky, a creature... She hadn't muddled through the rest yet.

And Terry wanted her to take Virginia's place. Wanted her to become this creature, this *Aswang*. In her mind she could picture an inquisitive baby chick, coal black, peering at her, cocking its head inquisitively.

What would it matter? She lived an empty, lonely life anyway.

Jemma stepped out into the early morning. Dogs barked and roosters crowed. The air smelled cool and clean, free of the heat and humidity that would come after the sun rose. The world was still cast in gray under a lavender cloudless sky. She wished for coffee. She knew she could go to the restaurant, or if she didn't want to, she could ask Alex to bring her some. But the idea she wasn't even in control of her life enough to get herself a coffee made her drop onto a bench overlooking the sea. She watched waves lapping at the shore. A fisherman landed his boat and carried in a net full of fish.

"Witch."

Jemma's heart pounded, blood rushed in her ears, but she simply turned her head to the newcomer.

There stood Anna. Her dark brown—almost black—eyes glittered with malice. "You should leave, witch. No one likes your kind here."

"You don't understand—"

"I understand you're a witch and you snoop in holy places you're better off not going to."

The first trappings of rage trickled in Jemma. She could hurt Anna. The mere thought made her set her jaw.

"Get away from me," she said.

"You'll leave today. Might come a time when you can't leave."

Jemma stood, facing her. Neither Jemma nor Anna were particularly tall, but Jemma had maybe an inch on the other girl. She took in the girl's tank top, her shorts. Anna didn't have to wear gloves. Didn't have to keep herself covered.

"I tell you this for your own good. We don't let witches live around here."

"Are you threatening me?" Jemma asked. She started to peel off her glove. Anna glanced at it, trying to keep the curiosity out of her gaze. This was a situation she did have power over. Finally, something she could control. If she became the *Aswang*, then everyone would fear her. She would have power over every situation.

"Not threatening. Telling. Leave El Nido. Leave this country. You're a witch."

Jemma almost faltered. If she was wrong about Anna, she would only hurt herself. But she wasn't wrong.

Jemma slapped the other woman. Not a hard slap. It didn't have to be. Relief, cool as the early morning breeze, washed into Jemma. She forgot about the man she'd been married to, forgot what he'd done to her as the sun pushed up over the mountains to the east. It changed the water from a mysterious gray to cheerful sparkling blue.

Anna clutched at her face and dropped to her hands and knees. She made a sound she'd maybe intended to be a scream, but it came out as a guttural, barking noise.

One of the nearby stray dogs trotted over, perhaps to investigate, but caught wind of something he didn't like and ran away with his tail between his legs.

Jemma embraced her sensation. Remembered the first time she'd felt this way, after she thrust a week of torture and three days of starvation into Alex. Watched him scream and writhe on the floor. The memory remained but it still wasn't connected. Didn't tug at her inside and make her hurt. She couldn't process what she'd done yet. She wondered what it would do to her when she could.

It didn't matter. It was worth it.

Anna seemed older. Lines stood out on her face where they hadn't before.

"Don't say a word to anyone about this," Jemma said.

Anna shook her head. Silent tears coursed down her cheeks.

Reluctant, Jemma pulled the glove back on. She made her way back to her cabin, and let herself in.

She didn't want victims. She never wanted to hurt anyone. It had seemed so easy. She could be a good *Aswang*. Could only eat cattle, or pigs. Look at the self-control she'd carried for years. She could think of it as insurance she would never be pushed around again.

Something moved outside her curtains. Alex slowly walked past, to see if she were awake yet. She opened the door and waved him in. She didn't want to tell him about Anna, but she had to. The other she would keep to herself.

"I hurt Anna," she said.

"Anna?"

"The kitchen girl. Who tends bar for Terry."

"Jesus, Jem. Where is she?"

"The beach. I didn't touch her for long, I slapped her."

Alex's eyebrows asked what the hell had happened on the

beach. "She called me a witch. She told me we had to leave or someone would kill us. That they didn't tolerate witches here."

"So you did the thing that made her call you a witch again, only this time you dumped all your shit onto her?"

Jemma nodded. He would never understand. What it was like to be trapped in herself, all day every day.

"What did you find out from Terry?" he asked.

"There are no ghosts on the island. What's on the island is Terry's wife Virginia. She got cancer, and he made her a ... the closest thing I can call it is vampire. He calls it an *Aswang*." Alex sat on the bed. The springs squeaked under his bulk. "It's behind the missing people. And why there are no ghosts. It eats them, sort of."

"We're leaving. Today."

"No!"

"You've been threatened once already and it's not even 6:45. We know how to talk to ghosts. I don't even know what the fuck a vampire is...alive? Dead? I don't want to know. I bet the poltergeist is still haunting Yonkers."

"We're not going."

For the second time this morning, Jemma swum with power. Most of it siphoned from others. But she had to get it where she could. She couldn't be powerless all the time.

"I'm calling the airline and getting us on the first fight we can manage. We can get the eleven a.m. van to Puerto, maybe stay there a night if we need to. We can't fight a vampire."

"She isn't a vampire, exactly."

"I don't care. Ghosts can't touch us. Can't hurt us. Can only mind-fuck us. I'm not dealing with a vampire."

"You're not curious?"

"No. And neither are you. Get packed, get your shit together, I want to be ready to go in an hour."

"It could be an all-new book."

"I don't care about books. He turned his wife into a monster."

"She was dying. She asked him to. She wanted to be with him. They had such a short time together, and she wanted more."

"And he did it?"

"It's a romantic notion."

"How did it work out?" Alex stood.

"Terrible."

"So why on earth do you want to get involved with something like this? We know ghosts."

I know ghosts, Jemma thought. Alex knew machines that measured the energy in the air, measured radiation. He could record sounds, photograph orbs. Jemma still didn't think orbs were anything more than dust on a lens.

"It's my book, right?" Jemma asked.

"Don't pull this bullshit."

"It's my book, if I want a vampire in it, we're doing the vampire."

"Don't be a spoiled brat."

This caught Jemma. The wave of euphoria started to subside. What else could she be beyond a brat? She resisted the urge to withdraw, to curl into a ball and weep.

"Please. It's important."

Alex ground his teeth, she could hear it.

"You saw the Chinese kid, Jem. The monster you want to go and look at did that."

I don't want to study it. I want to be it.

Alex sighed. "Why don't you take a rest?"

"I rested all day yesterday."

"You're exhausted."

"I feel fine. After Anna, I feel fantastic. I want to go to the island. What if we could find her in the daytime?"

"I won't let that happen." A new voice joined the conversation. Terry stood in the open doorway to the cabin. "After what you took from me, surely you understand."

Jemma knew this to be true. He would never hurt her. He dreamed of slipping away, back to England, and leaving her on the island. But a monster like Virginia needed a keeper to ensure she stayed in line. The townspeople held him to that duty.

"You both will stay right here until the evening. Then you want to meet my wife? I'll take you to her."

"I look forward to it," Jemma said.

Terry laughed, and closed the door behind him. A lock

clunked into place. Alex tried the door, but of course it didn't open. He could be so foolish sometimes.

Pain crept back into Jemma like water creeping through the bottom of a leaky boat. It rose steadily, reliably. Pain was her only constant. Pain and Alex. He tried the windows, but Mr. Lucky appeared outside, a machete tucked into his belt.

They were trapped. And it was all her fault. She shouldn't have hurt Anna.

"Any ideas?" she asked.

"Working on it. I could call Karen."

"Would she help?"

"I don't know. What do I say? I'm stuck in my beachfront cottage by a machete-wielding madman?"

"The townspeople all know about Virginia."

"What?"

"Haven't you felt the way they've looked at us?"

"I thought—" He paused, and she knew he felt he'd stuck his foot in his mouth. "I thought they just thought you dressed funny."

"It's all right. I thought that too." How else could she dress? No one could touch her.

"I'm going to call Karen."

"And what? We're thousands of miles from home. They knew we were coming when we stepped off the plane here. She couldn't get us past Mr. Lucky out there."

Jemma peered out the curtains. She hated him. He reeked of malice and evil. Another one of Virginia's keepers.

Alex took his phone out and thumbed a text message. Jemma wondered what he wrote.

They sat for a moment and listened to the morning. The temperature rose.

"You know what no one would expect?" Alex said.

Jemma bit back on a joke that had been played out long ago. "What?"

"You. Dressed like the average Palawan vacationer."

"Impossible."

"And if we found some colored tanning lotion, you wouldn't be so painfully white."

"I don't have any touristy clothes."

Alex pointed out behind her cottage. There hung a clothesline where the Vista Breeze staff hung tourists' laundry up to dry. "If you went up to Mr. Lucky, you could distract him."

"What are you talking about?"

"If you went up to him with no hat, no sunglasses, in shorts and a tank top."

The thought of such a thing made her heart pound.

"Go out there, ask him if he's doing tour C today, and when it's leaving. Flirt. Giggle."

"I can't. You *know* I can't."

"If you run for the clothes, change, I bet you can swipe some tanning stuff from the store," Alex mused.

"I'm not going out there."

"The other option is to be hand delivered to Terry's beloved."

"I'm sure we can think of something else…a better plan. What if you went?"

Alex shook his head. What if someone touched her? What if Mr. Lucky looked at her? Alex wanted it so he could see her skin…she rubbed at the baggy silk dress she wore. It soothed her, covered her, wrapped her in black. It kept her safe. In it she was a weird girl, nothing more.

Alex went to the bathroom, yanked the screen out of the window.

"I can see the clothesline," he said, upon his return. "A ton of stuff. Probably will fit you. And totally out of Lucky's sight lines."

"You go?"

"I can't fit through the fucking window. I'm a big dude."

"What if I can't get back in?"

"You're not supposed to get back in, babe."

Tears sprang to her eyes.

Jemma hugged herself. Ghosts were so much easier. Ghosts she could navigate. Mr. Lucky was a real man…men she couldn't handle.

"But he's real."

"I know he is."

"Slip out the window, grab some clothes, change in the

bushes. Then walk to the store and steal the colored tanning stuff. Put it on so you aren't so pale anymore. And so you don't get a sunburn. Then go talk to Mr. Lucky. While you distract him, I'm going to get out the front window."

"Then what?"

"Karen's boat."

That changed things. They would never make it to Puerto Princesa on one of the Jeepneys or vans…everyone knew everyone and it would be too easy to intercept them. But a boat? Maybe they could make it to the airport after all.

She wasn't giving up on the idea of meeting Virginia, but getting to another place to regroup safely wouldn't hurt. To research.

"Where will she meet us with the boat?"

"The beach in front of Merriweathers." The resort sat about a half mile down the beach. "We'll have to book it. Run like crazy and hope we're faster."

"I hate this idea," Jemma said.

"Do you see another way? I'm not going to sit here and let Terry take us to the island again."

"We could fight…"

"With what?"

Jemma kept silent. Alex was right. Maybe this was their best plan.

"Mr. Lucky's distracted. Now would be a good time to go. The window's open for you."

She couldn't even ask him for a boost. As with everything in the past ten years of her life, she needed to do this alone, too.

She hauled herself up to the small, high bathroom window, aware of how weak she was. As she squeezed through the window, her hip caught on something. The fabric of her dress tore with a growl. It didn't matter. She wouldn't wear it for long.

Jemma landed on the shadowy, soft dirt with a quiet thump. The wide moon of Alex's face appeared in the window. He didn't speak. She didn't either, not wanting to call attention to herself. She stood and brushed herself off. And examined the clothesline. There! A pair of jeans.

…but that wasn't what this disguise was about. She ought to

pick the articles that were the most repugnant to her. The ones she'd be least likely to wear.

A midriff-exposing halter-top. And a pair of black surf shorts that barely covered her ass cheeks. Even being out here without her hat and sunglasses threatened to push her into a panic attack. The thought of people seeing her legs, her arms, her stomach, her back...

It was funny; he hadn't left a single scar on her body. He did it on purpose, of course. Because he wanted to keep her pretty. He was the fool. She'd never been pretty.

Alex told her, once, that she had beautiful skin. She'd been curled in a chair and the leg of her pants had ridden up. She'd blushed, tried to erase the incident. Then he'd asked her why she bothered to shave her legs, and she'd almost cried with embarrassment. She still wanted to feel like a woman sometimes. She couldn't feel that way with hairy armpits, hairy legs.

Jemma darted out into the sunlit morning and took her prizes. She darted back into the shadow, hugging the damp warm wall of the cottage. Her heart pounded and blood thundered in her ears.

Now put them on.

The shorts were easy; she slid them on under the skirt. It had been over a decade since she'd worn something so tight. Constricting. Claustrophobic.

Now the scary part. She glanced up to make sure Alex wasn't looking. She couldn't see him. It's not that bad. Women do this every day.

Dressing like this is why he hurt you.

But she had never dressed like this! Never!

She whipped her torn dress off, and in her haste to cover up got caught in the halter-top. This was even worse, the idea that instead of seeing her dressed like a slut, someone would see her failing to dress like a slut, trussed and bound in her own clothes.

She fought with the shirt, tying it awkwardly behind her neck and behind her back. She imagined women asking their boyfriends and husbands to tie it for them. Like everything else, she would do this on her own.

"Can I look?" Alex whispered from above.

"I'd rather you didn't." She steeled herself. There would be time to curl into a ball later. To weep. To wrap herself in yards and yards of thick clothing. She didn't have shoes, but she guessed here that didn't matter.

"You need this." He flicked a hair elastic at her with half-intensity, so it merely glided to the ground at her feet. It wasn't hers. She found it in the bathroom when she got here. Her hair was all she had left to hide behind.

"Okay." She exhaled the word. Took a handful of her thick black hair and bound it in a sloppy ponytail. She blinked at the world, before her with no sunglasses, no hair to act as filter.

"Walk over like you own the place."

Acting. She studied it a bit in college. Had been quite good, everyone told her. She worried they were just being polite.

It didn't matter now. She pretended she wasn't terrified of the sun. Pretended she didn't care if people could see the delicate skin of her stomach. Like their visions could disembowel her. It made her shiver.

She saw no one as she walked to the store in the underside of the restaurant. There wasn't even anyone at the cash register. So she took a can of spray tan, and made her way back to the shadows behind the cottage. As simple as that. She selected what she wanted, reached for it, took it, and walked out. She saw no one. No one saw her.

Power?

It almost made her laugh as she resumed her place under Alex's window.

The orange caste of her skin amused her as she sprayed her legs. People paid money for this. Enjoyed it. Fascinating.

Alex, from the window, sprayed her back and her face.

She covered her arms, her underarms, her stomach.

"Now what do I do?" she asked.

"Go talk to him. Try and lead him to the beach."

"He'll know me."

"No. I don't even know you."

"Don't say that."

"You're totally different. Just...don't fold your shoulders

forward. Throw them back. Be proud."

"I'm not proud."

"You know that. I know because you tell me all the time. But no one else needs to know."

Jemma threw her shoulders back, aware of her breasts jutting out. All the more reason for people to look at her. She felt like a caricature of a woman, wanted to withdraw into her shell, a safe, warm Jemma snail.

She stole one final glance back at Alex, and steeled herself.

This was the first time she'd been in real danger in years. She hated the feeling.

She stepped out into the sun. Let it touch her skin.

Eleven years ago, she hadn't known what fear was. What pain was. She thought she did, sure. Everyone thinks they know. But once she felt real fear, thought she was going to die at someone else's hand...then she realized what a lovely life she'd been living.

When she talked to Mr. Lucky, she had to speak clearly. Couldn't mumble, couldn't talk to her shoes. She was a tourist. She was excited to be here. He was a tour guide; she wanted to see the places where he took people.

He sat on the stoop of her cottage, staring at his bare feet and the dusty ground. Jemma thought about what Terry told them, about stepping on terrible, poisonous things.

"'Scuse me." She hated the sound of her voice. Usually hated it, really hated it now, with this phony enthusiasm.

Mr. Lucky had to recognize her. How could he not?

"You do tours, right?"

"Yes, but not today. Today is a day off. A holiday."

"No way!" Jemma focused on every TV show she'd ever watched. Every movie she'd ever seen. "What's the holiday? Which boat is yours? Can we see it from here?"

She hoped the sweat pouring down her back didn't mess up the spray tan.

"You've not heard of the holiday. It is special here in El Nido."

"There gonna be parties tonight?" She focused the slight English accent out of her voice.

"There are parties every night here."

"Which boat is yours?" she asked again. "And which tour is best? There's three tours, right? So which one is best? Show me your boat!"

He stood, that was something. He drank her in with his eyes. The little shorts that sat on her hips, the slightest curve of her stomach.

He scrutinized her. He must know something was up. She had to get him away from the cottage.

"So if it's a holiday, then are any boats going out?"

"Some yes, some no."

"Can you show me which ones are going?"

"I cannot."

"Are you, like, busy or something?" God she sounded stupid. But lots of people sounded stupid, so maybe she wasn't so far off her mark.

"Yes, very busy."

She laughed. "Doing what? Sitting? It'll take four seconds. Take me to a tour guy, set me up, and you can come back to your stoop or whatever."

He might be considering it.

"You better be busy, 'cause you're missing all the money of that trip."

Mr. Lucky sighed, and peeked over his shoulder at Jemma's cottage door. She could imagine Alex crouched inside, listening for what came next.

"Five minutes," he said. "Let's go."

"Thank you so much. But you never told me which tour is best?"

Thinking of Lot's wife, Jemma didn't look back at her cottage. She kept her eyes forward, on the ever-changing cerulean seas.

Twenty-One

A lex pressed himself against the door, listening to the conversation outside. Jemma didn't sound entirely natural, but he wondered if anyone who didn't know her would pick up on it. He suspected not. Certainly Mr. Lucky wouldn't.

Their voices started to recede. One quick slam with his shoulder should take care of the flimsy lock. It was one of those things he'd never attempted, but always watched when heroes did it in the movies. He thought he could handle it. Hoped he could, anyway.

He hazarded a glance out the window, and couldn't see Jemma or Mr. Lucky. Go time.

Alex launched himself into the door. A crack, a sharp pain in his shoulder, but no movement. One more. It gave a little bit, but the whole process proved much louder than he'd anticipated. He wound up for a running start, bounced off the door again, and finished it off with a kick. His shoulder hurt like a motherfucker. The door flew open and smacked into the wall.

Karen should arrive in front of Merriweathers any minute now. A half-mile north down the beach. Toward town. He didn't much care for that. But beggars, it is said, can't be choosers.

A 230-pound dude has a hard time being secretive and sneaky pretty much anywhere. Yes, he was tall. Yes, he carried his weight well. But it still didn't make him a little dude. Didn't make it easy for him to cross the beach without being noticed.

He caught a glimpse of Jemma talking to Mr. Lucky. He should have grabbed one of her dresses for her, but on the other hand, she had the rest of her life to curl up in a burlap sack. He kept his head down, and tried to walk like a man with a destination. He wondered what Terry was doing.

A half-mile down the beach wasn't so far. He wished he could check on Jemma. He executed a casual, wide turn, hand shielding his eyes from the sun, hoping to look like a dude scoping the scenery, and nothing more. There was fantastic scenery to scope. He wished he had even the slightest chance to enjoy it. Vampires and being locked in cottages sort of bled the fun out of the lovely vistas.

He could see Jemma, as she made her way down the beach. She stopped to talk to a native boy. Well, it was un-Jemma. The Merriweathers resort sign featured a margarita glass, a palm tree, and a crescent moon, painted faded Day-Glo pink. Alex dropped into a wicker beach lounger, and stared out at the water. He examined each *Bangka* and motorboat. He hoped *Lucky Daze* could outrun *Baby Roxanne*. Once Mr. Lucky went back to the cottage, he'd see they were gone.

From his peripheral vision (god, he hoped he was being discreet) he watched Mr. Lucky leave the beach. Alex stood, willing Jemma to hurry the fuck up. Where was Karen? He'd stressed the gravity of the situation, so it wasn't as though she would get distracted and wander off. There were plenty of little boats out there, but most of them seemed to be unmanned, waiting in the early morning to collect tourists and head out into the islands.

Where was she?

Jemma moved down the beach at a casual, meandering pace. They had maybe three seconds before Mr. Lucky came after them. Would he put two and two together, or was Jemma's disguise solid?

Two things happened at once: Karen put-putted the *Lucky Daze* into view. A half-mile down the beach, Mr. Lucky came sprinting from the Vista Breeze resort, a tiny white Terry behind him.

Jemma ran.

Alex headed into the water toward Karen, the boat name gnawing at him. Running from Lucky to *Lucky* didn't quite sit right. Jemma saw him and cut into the water—which would slow her down, shit—to triangulate the distance.

Karen worked her boat in as shallow as she dared.

This, Alex reflected as his heart slammed against his ribs, is why people run for fun. So when the time comes to run for your life, it's not quite so painful.

Closer to the boat now, he paused and watched Jemma struggle through the calf-deep water.

Lucky closed the distance between them.

Alex waited, not sure if he should board the boat or go try and hold off Mr. Lucky. The man carried a machete, there wasn't much Alex could do.

A loud pop—gunshot?—rent the morning, and something splashed and exploded in front of Mr. Lucky, then blazed brilliant green. For a moment it glowed brighter than the sun.

Karen stood on the nose of her boat, wildly sexy in her conservative khaki shorts and button-down shirt, a neon orange flare gun in her hand.

It bought them the time they needed. Jemma came to him, and he stepped out of her way, letting her clamber gracelessly on board.

Karen extended a hand to help her, and Jemma muttered a terse "no thanks," then a harsher "please don't touch me."

"Go!" Alex flung himself into the boat with a wave of warm seawater.

Jemma curled into one of the seats, wrapping her arms around herself as best she could. Karen lobbed the flare gun to Alex, gawked at Jemma a little, and started the motor.

Alex pointed the gun at Mr. Lucky, who'd resumed his pursuit. He didn't want to shoot anyone. He wanted to get away. He fired another flare in front of his pursuer, and again, Mr. Lucky stopped. He shielded his eyes, and started to laugh.

"Not so lucky now, eh?" Alex called. The guy'd finally flipped his shit. Good. Now to get to Puerto, get on a plane, and get the hell out of here. Back to New York, back to snow and sleet and rude people. Back to home.

Jemma found a towel and wrapped herself in it.

"Are you guys okay?" Karen asked.

He nodded. How much to tell? *There's a vampire on Sakripisiyuhin Island, and once we found out about it, it was then time to leave, as our charming British resort owner was going to feed us to her?*

"We've not made friends."

"Was that Alastair Lucky?"

Alastair? Who would have imagined Mr. Lucky would have a first name. Or that his last name was actually Lucky?

"Yes. He's pretty pissed. He works for Terry Brenton, who's not the least bit impressed with our snooping."

"Huh," Karen said, and then turned her attention to the calm ocean waters. They rode along in silence, and Alex found himself almost lulled to sleep by the rhythmic motion of the speedboat. Faster than the *bangkas*, Alex wondered why all the tour guides didn't run these.

"Where are we going?" Jemma asked, pulling Alex from his thoughts.

Karen mumbled something, lost in the breeze.

"This is the island!"

Karen cut the engine, said, "Don't you touch me," to Jemma.

The cross of the island loomed over them. Jemma was right, of course. This was Sacrifice Island. The midmorning sun indicated they had plenty of time before Virginia came out of her hiding place.

"Why are we here?" Alex asked, his voice seeming way too loud in the silence left behind from the engine. Waves lapped at the boat and the shore in the protected beach cove, and the hull of the boat scraped the sand. Karen hopped out, and he watched the water swirl around her muscular calves as she tugged the boat in a little farther, then dropped the anchor.

She reached into the hull of the boat, and picked up the radio. Alex watched in stunned silence.

"I've got them here, over."

Static responded.

Jemma picked up a cooler and used it to bash the radio. Sparks flew, pieces skittered across the damp floor of the boat. She glared at Karen, the towel still looped over her shoulders.

Karen replaced the radio handset. "It doesn't matter. Get out."

"No way—" Jemma went for the outboard motor. Alex stood closer; he chastised himself for not thinking of it. She tugged at the starter, but was utterly unfamiliar with the operation of such things. By the time Alex collected his wits enough to help her, Karen pulled a petite, snub-nosed pistol from a concealed holster.

"Get out. Right now."

Alex gave the starter another tug, and she fired into the sky. A flock of birds erupted from nearby trees, shrieking and flapping.

"It's not worth dying over," Jemma said.

"Oh, I wouldn't kill you. Virginia would be angry if I did. I'd just shoot you in the leg, or somewhere where I'd be sure you'd survive till nightfall. Now get off my damn boat."

Jemma did. Around her ankles, the spray tan rinsed off, revealing alabaster skin underneath.

"Why?" he asked Karen as they disembarked.

"Neither of you have any idea what you got yourselves into. The night I met you, you were babbling about ghosts." Karen followed them ashore. "You can't simply come in and interfere with the top predator in an ecosystem. A tiger won't take more than she needs when things are in balance, it's when you force her hand, and make her come in contact with humans she becomes a man-eater. We've gotten used to having creatures like Virginia around. We know she needs to feed, and we know so long as she gets to in peace, she won't go on a rampage."

"He feeds her tourists."

"So what? Not enough so anyone notices."

"We noticed."

"Bullshit. You thought there were ghosts on this *haunted* island. It wasn't until you got here you saw people were missing. And no ghosts."

He couldn't argue.

Alex climbed up on the beach, baking in the midday sun. Jemma headed into the jungle, not even bothering with the well-trodden path. He needed to think. On the one hand, great that Jemma disabled the radio, but now they couldn't call for help if they needed it. He held his cell phone. At home, he knew to call 911. What the fuck do you call in the Philippines? And what the fuck do you call in a place where everyone is in bed with the monster?

Twenty-Two

Jemma's throat burned. Thirsty. She couldn't remember a time when she was thirstier, then she did, and she ignored it. She focused on the dry pain inside her. It made a nice reprieve from worrying about being barely dressed. She would have tried to take hold of Karen if she thought it would help...depending on the person she touched, it could be worse for them, or worse for her. Karen could feel guilty about this, could feel great. Jemma couldn't risk being incapacitated if Karen hurt worse than she did.

The shadows and pungent, earthy smells of the jungle enveloped her, and she felt better already. She couldn't blame Virginia for shirking the tropical sunlight.

"Why is she letting us wander away?" Alex asked.

"Why wouldn't she? Mr. Lucky and Terry are coming, I'm sure. We can't get off the island, she controls the only boat. Virginia, I'm sure, will be able to find us quite easily when dark comes. What does she care if we wander in and get a drink?"

They passed the dormitory, lower windows were dark, the upper windows reflected palm trees and sun. Was Virginia lurking in her basement nest, waiting for the sun to sink so she could hunt? Should Jemma go on in, confront her there?

The sound of water coursing over stones melted together with the sound of wind through the trees. She needed to drink first. The stream they'd heard when Mr. Lucky abandoned them here. She headed through the jungle, Alex, exasperated, on her heels.

The stream ran red. It wasn't much of one, barely more than a trickle of water through the rocks. But it ran the color of blood.

"I never thought we'd find it," she said. "And we don't have a camera. No one will believe us."

Alex stared at the stream for a few minutes. "I'm sorry. This is my fault."

"How is this your fault? How could you have known?" Of course it wasn't his fault.

"Incomplete research."

"I twisted the data to be what I wanted it to be. An island where people were afraid to go? Must be ghosts. We made it fit. It made sense. I didn't realize vampires were real." She laughed. It sounded silly, said out loud in the sunlight.

If she didn't laugh, she would cry. In Terry's mind, she saw a weapon. A particular kind of bamboo the *Aswang* is sensitive to. She scanned the jungle. Stood, marched forward in search of it.

Alex fumbled after her.

There.

"Do you have a knife?"

"Always—why do you ask?"

It wasn't a big knife. Wouldn't be of any use against, say, Karen or an *Aswang*, but it would, given enough time, cut through this bamboo and sharpen it down to a point.

"Give it to me."

"Why?"

"I need to make myself a *bagacay*."

Twenty-Three

Something watched from the shadows. Drawn by voices, Virginia emerged from her basement nest and followed the ghost hunters. She clung to cool, moist patches of darkness. She watched them at her red stream. The woman stared at the red water, the man held his head in his hands. She calculated. Take them now, risk being drawn out into the sun? Or wait. Terry promised to bring them to her. Promised to end this ridiculousness. What if she waited and they got on a boat and left again?

The bright sun bled her strength, but she crept closer. Hungry. She wanted to taste them. Something about the woman intoxicated her. The man would go first, and she would take her time with the woman.

Twenty-Four

Alex struggled to think of a way to get them off this island before nightfall. Jemma listened to the shadows, pointing, and frowning, unable to spot whatever she thought she heard. As the day advanced, the shadows stretched. She carried her sharpened bamboo spear. He didn't remember what she'd called it. He had no intention of being here when night fell.

"I'm going after Karen and her boat."

"It's not safe," Jemma said. "Stay here. Better to fight with Virginia than Karen."

That was bullshit. He'd much rather tussle with flesh and blood than a creature he didn't realize existed until the day before.

"She's already terrified of you. I think you can distract her while I get her gun away."

"I'm tired of distracting people."

"You're really good at it." Everyone always underestimated Jemma. Most of all, Jemma.

She frowned, but stood up, holding tight to her stick. Out in the sunlight, her skin seemed to glow. She wasn't hugging herself or covering herself quite so much. She'd get sunburn if she stayed out on the beach for long. They'd need to do something for the ride to Puerto, assuming he could commandeer the boat.

Alex followed her, wondering what she would do. For years she'd seemed so predictable, but this danger awakened a new desperation in her. It excited him.

Jemma marched out on the beach. "How much longer do we have to sit around here and wait?" she demanded.

Karen sat up from where she'd been relaxing in the sand,

cool in the shadow of one of the overhanging cliffs. "Nightfall."

"And you're just babysitting us?"

"Only until Terry arrives."

Karen started to back away from Jemma. Jemma held out her hands, sort of resembling a movie zombie. If vampires were real, were zombies real, too?

"Get away from me," Karen barked, and pulled out the gun. Jemma paused, but Alex went in for the kill. As he sprinted across the sand, he hoped he wouldn't have to kill her. He'd tackle her, take her down, get the keys...he remembered her underneath him the night before and wished it wasn't happening like this.

The echo of the gunshot ricocheted off the tall cliffs, thundering long after the damage was done. Birds took flight from the trees.

Alex's first thought was panic: Karen shot Jemma. Then he found himself falling forward, his legs all tangled and clumsy, unwilling to work. He landed with a mouthful of sand, and the impact brought out a pain in his gut.

It took a moment for it all to add up. He nearly spat out a laugh when he realized she'd shot *him*.

At least Jemma was okay. Better than okay. She came to him and hovered over him; she started to reach for him, then pulled back. He rolled himself onto his side and flopped onto his back. Hot, blinding pain radiated from his stomach, yet there a distance opened between him and the pain. A distance between him and everything. It was kind of nice, cottony and stuffed tight in the warm, sunny afternoon. His eyes slid closed, and he heard Jemma call his name. He forced them open and saw her lean over him.

"Don't go," she said.

"Maybe I'll stay with you. When I'm a ghost." He was dying. He didn't see any reason to fight it. It simply was. When he saw the blood in the sand, it made sense.

"Push on it," Jemma said. "I don't have anything to..."

Without a hint of resentment, Alex wondered if she had been dressed like normal if her long skirts could have saved him by making a compress. He'd never know.

"I love you," he told her.

"I love you, too." She wiped away tears with the heels of her hands.

"No, Jemma, I'm in love with you. My heart beats for you." It sounded so corny. He smiled. Poor heart, running out of things to pump.

"Kiss me," he said.

"I can't!" She gaped down at him, beautiful even under the layer of tanning lotion.

"It'll be okay, I promise." And it would be. He knew how her terrible gift worked. When she touched someone, pain traveled from the person with the most pain to the person with the least. And Jemma was always in pain. Right now, the cottony stuffing feeling kept his at bay. If he got a kiss, he'd never have another bad thought.

"I promise," he said again. "Please?"

"What if it—"

He cut her off.

"Please?"

He knew she worried; she'd be all fucked up and in agony if she received the pain of a gunshot wound. But she wouldn't. He knew it. He'd make her feel fantastic.

The gauze thickened. All the edges of the world were soft, cushioned. He couldn't feel anything now. The sound of the water on the beach became muffled, the sand under him felt like a featherbed. Everything was white and getting whiter. Was this the light everyone talked about? Would he finally see a ghost?

"Hurry."

She sobbed over him, and he wanted to apologize for hurting her. She leaned in.

Their lips touched. For a half second it was perfect. He kept his smile as the agony hit him full on. But he'd been ready for it. And it didn't matter, because it pushed him over the edge, gave him the gentle nudge from life into death.

Twenty-Five

"Alex?" Jemma cried his name over and over. She felt the moment his spirit left him. Selfishly, she wanted him to stay near her, to keep watch over her as he'd done in life. She didn't want him moving on to "a better place" if it meant losing him.

She hated that his kiss made her feel better, alive and sharp. Dumping the pain twice in one day made her feel like a person again. More than she had in years, since this all began. A fitting end for this phase of her life.

She turned to Karen.

"You did this to him."

Karen pointed the gun at Jemma. Her hands shook. The stark sunlight bleached her face white.

The sound of a boat took their attention. The *Baby Roxanne*, carrying Terry and the despicable Mr. Lucky. Relief washed over Karen's face, and Jemma took the opportunity to rush forward, heft her *bagacay*, and thrust it through Karen's chest.

She dropped in a heap in front of Jemma.

Jemma stood like a caged animal, holding her sharpened stick. Blood, darker than Jemma expected, coated it.

She wouldn't give up without a fight. She needed to find Virginia. She resisted the urge to kick Karen's slumped, traitorous body, for it wouldn't do anything except facilitate a transfer of pain. Jemma felt good right now; Alex's final gift served her well.

She turned and darted into the jungle.

Cool shadows wrapped around her partially clad body like a lover's embrace. She welcomed it.

She needed a plan. Think. Think. Tears sprang to her eyes. She'd kept Alex at her fingertips for years so she wouldn't have to come up with plans...she tossed out ideas, he crafted them into things. Like her book. If she lived, the book couldn't be completed without his help. She couldn't save herself. She was doomed to repeat history, strapped bare to a table, unable to do anything but die without outside assistance. Without Alex's assistance. Which is why her plan made sense, now more than ever.

She knew he loved her. She'd always known. It brought a hot shame to her face (more than the sunburn), a deep gnawing shame that was a part of her ever-present pain. She was sorry, but she didn't know how she could have loved him back without touching him.

"You're crying."

Jemma jumped, a girlish, embarrassing squeal eked from her lips.

Something spoke from the spaces between the wide jungle leaves. A lizard skittered away. Jemma realized the afternoon had fallen silent, no birds chirped overhead.

"Are you the ghost hunter?"

Not anymore, Jemma thought. I am nothing. Nothing without my friend who picked me up and made me a person. But not for long.

"Yes," she said.

A throaty chuckle.

"You're never going to leave this island."

"I know," Jemma said.

"Come here, girl."

Gladly.

Jemma walked toward the sound of the voice, pushing palm fronds out of her way.

On the bank of the red stream, Virginia appeared like a Cheshire cat: grin first. The rest of her faded into existence before Jemma's eyes. Beautiful, long auburn hair, dressed in a plain brown dress that would have looked at home on a World War Two wife. Her eyes weren't right, though. They were a predatory yellow, and they were hungry. "Virginia," Jemma said. "It's nice to finally meet you."

She laughed, and her smile wasn't right either. The skin around it seemed too elastic, the teeth too sharp. Jemma supposed it would have to be. Somewhere inside this creature huddled a black chick. A tiny, baby chicken. An undead, eternal thing that provided all the power.

Jemma hefted the *bagacay*.

"What do you intend to do with that?" The creature swayed rhythmically, just a little, like a snake trying to hypnotize its prey.

"I want to be you."

Virginia laughed again, a nasty, hollow sound.

"I want to be the next *Aswang* of Sacrifice Island."

"You don't."

"Why not?"

"You can't imagine the loneliness."

Now it was Jemma's turn to laugh.

"I can," she said. "I got married in college." Jemma sat on a rock, feeling the mossy stone on her bare legs. The red stream babbled happily in the background. "To a man I loved. He loved me, too, but he wasn't well. He was paranoid. He thought I had demons in me. Maybe I did."

Virginia folded in on herself, settling in to hear Jemma's story.

"He used to hit me and call me a temptress. He tried to fornicate the demon out of me. That didn't work either. Finally he tied me to a table in our basement. He thought he could bleed the demon out if he cut my throat. I touched—kicked him—and all the pain he'd caused me exploded out of me and into him. And it killed him. I lay tied to the table for four days before Alex found me." Alex. He was gone. What would she do without Alex? "Ever since then, I've not been able to touch another soul without transferring my pain to them, or taking their pain into me." Jemma didn't back down from Virginia's yellow eyes. "So you tell me about loneliness. I lived among them, never able to interact or be one with them. Living on a quiet island feels like heaven."

"You take pain?"

"Or I give it."

"Touch me."

"Are you miserable?"

"Very," said Virginia. "Perhaps you can take it from me."

"All right."

Virginia reached out her hand. A perfectly regular hand. Or so it seemed at first. But, like a Magic Eye, the longer Jemma looked, the more she could tell it wasn't right. The nails were too thick and too yellow. The texture of the skin more resembled scales than anything human.

Jemma clamped on to the creature's hot, dry wrist.

For a moment nothing happened.

Then Jemma took the *bagacay* and speared Virginia through the chest.

She made a whistling, wheezing sound like a tea kettle, and seemed to deflate.

The chick would come out her mouth.

Jemma got down on her hands and knees and waited. She let a beat pass before she pawed at the lifeless lips.

Underneath the sound of the rustling trees, she heard a faint "peep peep" from inside the emaciated form. Jemma clasped Virginia's jaw and pulled. It came off in her hand, the blood inside powdery and dry, and she tossed it aside. She reached a hand down the monster's throat and came up with a tiny chick that fit nicely in her hand. Its downy black feathers were slick with ichor. Button-black eyes blinked up at her. It peeped, a question.

She needed to swallow this thing.

She could easily crush it with the *bagacay*, spear it and destroy it. While it sat small in her hand, it would be huge to force down her throat. She hesitated.

Jemma opened her mouth as wide as she could. She heard her jaw pop.

At least Alex didn't have to see it, to know what she did.

The little bird tasted dank and ancient, like mold from a basement that's never seen the sun. Feathers tickled her tongue and she gagged, stomach protesting against this invasion. She fought it down, worried the muscles of her throat would constrict and destroy it and it would rot there and kill her.

But it passed, leaving a nasty, stale aftertaste.

Jemma sat. Distant waves crashed against the shore. Wind sang through the trees. The brook wasn't far off.

Then it all went quiet.

Jemma struggled to stand. The shadows grew deeper, like a time-lapse video of dusk, despite it barely being past noon.

Darker, darker, and as it grew darker, Jemma realized she couldn't feel her feet, her legs, her hands, or her hair.

Was this what Alex felt when he died?

She was becoming nothing.

The darkness swallowed everything, and Jemma ended.

Twenty-Six

Terry watched Jemma stagger away. Watched her crumple under an overhanging stone shelf, seeking cool darkness. He remembered when it had been his sweet, loving wife who'd been the one crawling off into the shadows.

Virginia lay on a patch of sand near the stream, curled into a frail ball, her face broken. He remembered when Rebecca St. Germaine's face looked very similar. When he touched her, the skin felt cold. He looked down upon the Virginia he remembered from the final time he brought her here, too thin, lines of worry and pain etched on her forehead. But she looked human.

He didn't dare wonder about her soul. He knew what his late wife believed, and he hoped it wasn't so. If it was, it meant she would burn in hell forever.

He liked to think there was more to it than that.

He stroked her cheek.

This meant he could go. Back to England. Home.

The orange sun sank lower in the sky. Mr. Lucky came to them, started to speak, but instead took in the tableau. Terry, cradling Virginia. Jemma nowhere to be found.

He turned and vanished into the jungle.

Some minutes later, he heard a boat's engine start up. That was all right, Terry told himself, there was still Karen's boat. Mr. Lucky was a savvy guy, though, he'd tow the *Lucky Daze* behind the *Baby Roxanne*, and Terry would never see either boat again.

Terry scooped Virginia's body in his arms and carried her to the beach. It was the first she'd been in the sun in a long time. They sat by Karen—Terry couldn't precisely tell if she was dead, and decided he didn't care. They were all dead. For Jemma would be hungry. He settled in on the sand and stroked Virginia's wispy white hair. And he waited.

Epilogue

The headache woke her, but the dryness and pain in her throat descended and consumed her as soon as she was conscious. Darkness surrounded her like a robe, and Jemma pulled it on in a way she'd never been able to before. She was hungry. Standing up was easy. Her limbs felt elastic, energized, and mobilized by starvation. Her tongue sat thick and dry in her mouth.

But there was food. She could smell it. The branches and vines of the jungle seemed to part for her, yield as she passed. This was her home, and she reigned as queen of her domain. There were interlopers here. For her to punish and consume.

She ran her hands over her taut flesh and snickered at the gauzy memories of her past modesty. Her body was fluid now. Could be anything she desired.

Jemma was hungry, and she strode forth into the night, toward the dark beach, to claim her prize.

About the *Aswang*

I've taken some liberties with the *Aswang* legend for this book. In popular Filipino folklore, the *Aswang* is an evil, vampire-like creature which feeds off humans. The legend varies all around the Philippines, with some interesting geographical differences. I've chosen to focus on the *mananangal* (viscera sucker) portion of the legend, the one that's most similar to our vampires. *Aswang* are usually female, but they can be either gender. They have human origins, and can be created one of four ways: ritual, communication, contamination, or heredity. Both ritual and communication involve the transference of a black egg or a black chick into the body. A person can be cured of being an *Aswang*, though it becomes more challenging the longer she's been an *Aswang*—the black chick must be purged and destroyed with fire. When the chick is coughed up, it will try to make its way back to the *Aswang*'s mouth.

Legend holds that an *Aswang* has a human form in the day, but at night it transforms into a monster. Traditionally they could fly, but I wanted my *Aswang* trapped on the island, so I took that talent away. The *Aswang* will locate a victim and drain their blood. They particularly enjoy draining unborn children. Sometimes they snatch babies from the crib. The *Aswang* isn't picky, and sometimes chooses to feast on the newly dead. It is said to remove corpses from places of mourning and replace them with bewitched banana trunks, which resemble the dead. It is particularly fond of liver.

Aswangs can be destroyed with a precise strike with a bolo or a sharpened bamboo stick called a *bagacay*. The creature has to be hit where it cannot reach its wounds, as its saliva will heal it instantly. You can keep an *Aswang* away with garlic or salt—remember that next time you vacation in the Philippines.

About the Author

If it screams, squelches, or bleeds, Kristin Dearborn has probably written about it. She revels in comments like "But you look so normal…how do you come up with that stuff?" A life-long New Englander, she aspires to the footsteps of the local masters, Messrs. King and Lovecraft. When not writing or rotting her brain with cheesy horror flicks (preferably creature features!) she can be found scaling rock cliffs, zipping around Vermont on a motorcycle, or gallivanting around the globe.

Kristin is the author of *Whispers, Stolen Away, Woman in White, Sacrifice Island,* and *Trinity.* She has also written several short stories, most recently appearing in *Chopping Block Party: An Anthology of Suburban Terror, Screaming Cacti,* and *Single Slices Volume 1.* Learn more about her at www.kristindearborn.com.

Curious about other Crossroad Press books?
Stop by our site:
http://store.crossroadpress.com
We offer quality writing
in digital, audio, and print formats.

www.ingramcontent.com/pod-product-compliance
Lightning Source LLC
Chambersburg PA
CBHW030233180626
46810CB00008B/3105